CHALLENGE
AT
CASTLE GAP

Challenge at CASTLE GAP

Ben Douglas

Sunstone Press
Santa Fe, New Mexico

FIRST EDITION
Printed in the United States of America

Library of Congress Cataloging in Publication Data:

Douglas, Ben 1912-
    Challenge at Castle Gap

    I. Title.
PS3554.O8233C5   1984   813'.54   83-20216
ISBN: 0-86534-043-9

Published in 1984 by Sunstone Press / Post Office Box 2321 / Santa Fe, New Mexico 87504-2321 / USA

To my wife Barbara,
and to our children,
whose support and encouragement
made this book possible.

CHAPTER 1

She had been the only passenger to leave the train. There was no one in sight around the station although she could see the ticket agent inside clacking away at his telegraph key. Grandfather Ballantine's letter had been explicit. He would meet her train on this date at 2:15 in the afternoon. The train had been only ten minutes late.

Although it was May with summer several weeks away, it seemed to Jamie that the sun shone more fiercely than it ever did back in Missouri. What would it be like in August? Intolerable probably. But then she had not promised her grandfather to stay longer than a couple of months.

Her train was pulling out now and, as she stood alone on the station platform watching it recede into shimmering heat waves, she could not escape the feeling that her entire life up to that moment was departing with it.

A chilling thought struck her. Suppose she had gotten off at the wrong station? She glanced up at the weathered sign above the passenger entrance to the waiting room. GOODLAND. The person who selected that name must have been, she thought, an incurable optimist or a practical joker. There was no mistake. She was in the right place at the right time.

There was nothing to do but wait.

She picked up her two suitcases and carried them into the station, selecting a seat on the bench nearest the door. It was dusty. From what she had heard and read it was probable that everything in west Texas was perpetually dusty.

Someone had left a newspaper on the bench. It was three days old: May 11, 1912. There were several interviews with survivors of the *Titanic* disaster and she fell to reading them.

The sinking of the *Titanic* had passed almost unnoticed by Jamie Ballantine, coming as it did only two days after the deaths of her parents in a grade crossing accident near the edge of Kansas City. They had driven the fifty miles to the city in a desperate, last-ditch attempt to obtain new financing for the failing family business, a deteriorating small-town hotel.

The stories of the *Titanic* survivors held Jamie's attention only briefly. In a sense, she was a survivor of disaster, too. The only survivor since she had no brothers or sisters or uncles or aunts, either. Jamie's father had been an only child. There had been her mother's older sister but she never married and died early in life. Her maternal grandparents were also gone.

If it were not for her grandfather Ballantine she would have been alone at the funeral. Yes, there were friends and the Reverend Burkett had been helpful and understanding. But not the same as family. The surge of emotion that filled her when her grandfather put his arm around her shoulders as the caskets were being lowered into the ground came back to her.

In the three or four days following, her grandfather had busied himself with making arrangements for probate of her parents' estates, retaining an attorney and making an inventory of the assets. Things were worse than Jamie had thought. The hotel was mortgaged for as much as it was worth and the furnishings and other personal property had been put up as security for a private loan. All had to be sold to satisfy the obligations. Little would remain – probably only enough to pay the attorney. Jamie realized that all she had was a small life insurance policy, only $3,000. Her grandfather had made arrangements with the attorney to collect this for her.

Jamie remembered her conversation with her grandfather a few days after the funeral services. He had said that circumstances at the ranch made it necessary for him to return as quickly as possible and besides, things were about as well under control as he could manage. The attorney would take care of the details. Then he had suggested that she come out to the ranch for a month or so as soon as the estate proceedings were underway. A change of scenery and a new perspective would be helpful, he had said.

Well, why not. There was nothing to keep her. At twenty-two, she had received her fine arts degree in January but had not yet found a teaching position. There seemed to be a considerable surplus of music teachers. And the idea of visiting the Ballantine ranch intrigued her. She had never been there although her father had made several trips and had described it in detail.

Jamie glanced at the clock in the stationmaster's office: 2:49. She had just decided to wait until 3 o'clock before going into town when a yellow Oldsmobile touring car escorted by a choking cloud of brown dust came to a halt with a squeal of brakes in the gravelled road alongside the station.

John Bowie Ballantine stepped out, slapping dust from his jacket as he strode into the station. He was wearing rancher's clothing with a fine pearl-grey Stetson hat and brown, high-heeled boots. She hurried

8

to meet him.

The delay, her grandfather explained, had been caused by a flat tire. Something to do with a thorn from a prickly pear, whatever that was. The land sounded hostile already, Jamie thought.

After leaving the station, the road crossed the tracks and immediately left the edge of town heading south toward the Ballantine ranch some forty miles away. One could scarcely call it a road, she thought. It was little more than a pair of wheel tracks winding an uncertain way through mesquite, sage and cactus.

"Only two ranches between town and Bien Escondido," her grandfather was saying. "Just takes too many acres to support one critter. But that keeps the price of land cheap, even now. I'm ashamed to tell you how little I paid for my five thousand acres in '89."

"Is ranching all there is here?" Jamie asked. "I mean, aren't there any minerals or something like that? Nothing else for people to do?"

'No, at least not now. But some of us hope that someday there may be petroleum or other discoveries. We've had no exploration to this point."

They were travelling over fairly level terrain with only an occasional arroyo to cross. About an hour after leaving Goodland and perhaps thirty miles out of town, Jamie saw some low hills rising on the southern horizon, the only landmark to break the monotony. She called her grandfather's attention to them.

"Well, Jamie," he said, "what you see is Castle Mountain. It was a mighty important piece of geography in these parts sixty, seventy years ago – a sort of aiming point for travellers on the Chihuahua Trail from east Texas to Chihuahua City in old Mexico. The Butterfield stages came down that trail on their way to California. In fact, almost everybody who wanted to go west or southwest in this part of Texas had to take the same trail."

"You see," her grandfather continued, "the Pecos river was a considerable barrier to travel in those days. Crossings that could be negotiated by freight wagons or by stages were very far between. One of the most important was Horsehead Crossing about fifteen miles west of Castle Mountain. The trails came from the east through Castle Gap which you will see in a few minutes and went west to Horsehead Crossing."

Jamie considered the distant Castle Mountain profile for a moment. She thought of the Missouri Ozarks where she had been on summer vacations. Somehow, she had the impression that everything in Texas was outsized. Mountains should be too, she thought. But this Castle Mountain was no more than a medium-sized hill.

As they moved southward, it came into view. Castle Gap was a cleft or low saddle between the north and the south portions of the "mountain" which she guessed to be four or five hundred feet higher than the level ground to the west.

Her grandfather stopped the car. "We're almost home but I want to take a minute to show this to you." He was out of the car now pointing to the ground next to the road. "Only a few places left where you can see the marks of the old stage road and this is one of them. Most of the ruts and tracks are washed or blown away."

It had required a considerable mixture of faith and imagination to make out the old trail, she realized, but to have done otherwise would have disappointed her grandfather.

A few hundred yards beyond the crossing they came to the ranch entrance. Two large fieldstone columns flanked the road topped by a large wooden sign. BIEN ESCONDIDO, it proclaimed and under that, J.B. Ballantine. Her grandfather explained that the gateway did not mark the boundary of the ranch. They had been on Ballantine land for more than a mile.

Jamie could see the ranch house now. There were several other buildings and a couple of corrals. Two windmills were slowly turning. Beyond the house was a small lake.

"Welcome to Bien Escondido," her grandfather said bringing the car to a stop in front of the house. "I see the reception committee has assembled."

Two women stood on the low porch that ran along the east side of the house. Jamie recognized them immediately from her grandfather's descriptions. The older woman, in her fifties, was Ruth Hazelton. She had been Mr. Ballantine's housekeeper since a year or so after Mrs. Ballantine had died in 1904. The younger one was Annie Murphy who probably did most of the actual housework, Jamie thought. Her grandfather had said that Annie was not the brightest person in west Texas but a good worker and honest.

Mrs. Hazelton came down the steps and extended her hand. "We're so glad to have you here, dear," she said. "Come on in out of the sun right away. Annie will bring your luggage."

The coolness and relative darkness of the long living room were welcome as was the lemonade Annie brought. Mrs. Hazelton apologized for the lack of ice. They had it occasionally, she said, but it came from town and was usually half melted when it arrived. "Our life is not exactly Spartan but there are a lot of things we just have to get along without."

The description of her train trip from Kansas City occupied the next half-hour. It was Jamie's longest journey and had been full of interesting experiences. Two Indians had "invaded" the train at a watertower stop, but only for the purpose of offering some beaded moccasins for sale. A travelling salesman, in the hour that he was on the train, spent thirty minutes extolling the virtues of the Majestic Kitchen Range and the other thirty minutes describing how he had been "right next to Teddy Roosevelt all the way up San Juan Hill."

Her grandfather had questions about the closing of the estates and disposition of the remaining assets which Jamie answered as best she could.

It was now 5:30 and Mrs. Hazelton suggested that Jamie might like to rest for an hour or two before supper. "And by the way," she said, "the evening meal in Texas is always supper — never dinner." *What does she think we call it in Missouri?* Jamie wondered.

The upstairs bedroom that was Jamie's during her visit was not as hot as she imagined it would be and she soon fell asleep. *I'm home,* she thought as she drifted off.

CHAPTER 2

"There's something I don't understand, grandpa," Jamie said. "Since you don't run cattle here anymore – just lease the land to a neighboring outfit – why don't you close the house and move into town where life would be easier?"

Her grandfather thought a moment before answering. "I suppose you might say I'm part of the land, now. Been here too long to want to be anywhere else. And your grandmother is buried here on the ranch. She's part of it now forever. I'm happy here. Don't think I would be anywhere else."

Supper finished, they were sitting on the east porch looking over the lake and on to Castle Gap where the sun still caught the top of the hill. Mr. Ballantine was enjoying an evening cigar and the only sound other than their voices came from the kitchen where Annie was finishing the dishes.

"Something else, grandpa. The name of the ranch. Bien Escondido.

It means, if I'm correct, 'well hidden.' But it isn't hidden at all. You can see it for half a mile in any direction and, I suppose, three or four miles from the high ground east."

He formed three small smoke rings and examined them intently as they drifted away before replying.

"You might say it was your grandmother's idea. I didn't bring her out here until the house was finished in 1890. It would have just been too rough, living in a tent and out of the back of a wagon.

"When I did bring her – it was about the first of September – she took a long look at the place and said, 'I certainly hope the Lord knows where we are. It's so well hidden that surely nobody else does.' She was referring, you see, to the remoteness of the house. As a joke we started calling it the 'well hidden' ranch which grew into Bien Escondido."

"How did you and grandma ever happen to come here?"

"Several reasons. Mostly because people were getting too close together back in Austin to suit me. I like a place where I can whoop and holler as loud as I wish and no neighbor will complain.

"Land could be bought very cheaply here twenty-five years ago and it seemed like the time to get in at the bottom. As I said earlier, I'm almost ashamed to tell you the price I paid for my original five thousand and I practically stole the additional twelve thousand acres that I picked up in 1895. Times were hard, then. Very hard.

"There was another reason, too," he went on. "I had an idea then, back in 1889, that a railroad might come through Castle Gap and on across the Pecos. It was based only on the knowledge that the old trail and the stage roads came that way. And buffalo used the same route in their migrations. When the Union Pacific was laid out across Nebraska and Wyoming in the 1860s it followed old buffalo migration routes much of the way.

"If the railroad had come that way it would have crossed Ballantine land and the value of the ranch would have quadrupled. But it didn't happen. The railroad went north of us. Anyway, I had made a good bit of money on some land deals that were either shrewd or lucky – maybe a little of both – and I was getting tired of Austin. It looked like an adventure to come out here and happily your grandmother was the adventurous type too."

It sounded reasonable, Jamie thought, although she had a few mental reservations about her grandmother having been so agreeable to the idea. Had she been in grandmother's shoes, she was sure she would have been skeptical about such an inhospitable place.

Jamie was left with the feeling, which lacked any valid explanation, that the pieces did not fit together precisely. Something in her grandfather's explanation troubled her but it was impossible to place a finger on it.

Mrs. Hazelton had not entered into the conversation between Jamie and her grandfather but she spoke now, changing the subject. "Have you told Jamie about our other summer guest, John?" she asked.

Mr. Ballantine's cigar was out and he touched a match to it before replying. "Well, Jamie, it's a young man. His name is Dick Thatcher. I'd guess him to be about twenty-five. He's an instructor or assistant professor – I can't ever remember which – at some small college in east Texas

"Seems as though he's an amateur anthropologist or archaeologist. Doesn't make much difference which, I guess. He's interested in pre-Indian culture and has some sort of idea that the Castle Gap area is a good place to look for evidence. Because it had been a natural migration route. Can't say that I agree with him but he seems determined.

"Thatcher came out here for a week or so last summer and took a look around. Said he liked the prospects and would come back this summer if he had my permission. I guess I took a liking to the man. Anyway, I invited him to come on out and make his headquarters here at Bien Escondido. He insists on paying something for board and room which I don't want but he won't have it any other way. He'll be here on the 28th and we'll be driving in to pick him up then.

"You see, Jamie, when I made these arrangements with Thatcher, I had no idea things would happen in Missouri the way they did. I hope his being here won't inconvenience or disturb you in any way."

"Grandpa, if you like the man," Jamie replied, "that's all the recommendation necessary. We'll get along fine, I'm sure."

She thought, *what an interesting development! Why hasn't he said something about this earlier! Does the old rascal imagine himself to be a potential match-maker!* She looked at her grandfather closely to see if any facial expression might offer a clue.

But Mr. Ballantine's eyes were following the slow ascension of two more perfectly formed smoke rings.

Mrs. Hazelton spoke again. "And, Jamie, you'll soon be meeting another one of our little family here at the ranch: Morgan Black. Dr. Morgan Black, that is. He lives in Goodland but spends a lot of time out here. So much so that it's a second home. He has his own bedroom, in fact. Your grandfather and Dr. Black have played at least ten thousand games of checkers and dominoes."

"Doesn't he have any family in Goodland?" Jamie asked.

"He never married," her grandfather said. "Planned to a long time ago, but his fiancee died from some sort of fever. I don't know the details; he doesn't talk about it. I guess he never got over it. He's pretty well retired from active practice of medicine. There are a couple of younger doctors in town who take care of things. Texans don't get sick very often."

Surely this has to be the end of 'our little family' at the ranch. Where will they all stay? she wondered. Taking a quick mental inventory from her brief trip through the house that afternoon, they must be one or two bedrooms short.

As if she had read Jamie's mind, Mrs. Hazelton explained. "You've already been to your room, Jamie. Mine is next to it and John's is at the north end of the hall. Annie has the room at the other end of the hall. Dr. Black sleeps in John's den downstairs when he stays overnight at the ranch. And Mr. Thatcher, when he gets here, will have what used to be the foreman's room in the bunkhouse. We've fixed it up to serve as an extra bedroom if needed."

A brief silence followed broken only by the appearance of Annie who announced that her work was finished and she was going to bed.

"Please light the lamp in Miss Ballantine's room when you go up," Mrs. Hazelton said. Nodding assent, Annie left the porch and started upstairs. Jamie heard one of the steps squeak under her feet.

Jamie found herself staring through the darkening twilight at the deep cleft of Castle Gap on the eastern horizon. She thought of the thousands of historical vignettes which had passed that way. The Butterfield Stage Lines to California, for example, in the 1850s. Who might have been aboard? People headed for the goldfields, surely. Gamblers, women of questionable virtue, teachers and preachers. A cross-section of an opening frontier. Long before that, Spanish conquistadores, perhaps. And her grandfather had said that buffalo had migrated through the gap probably in herds of thousands. She closed her eyes and imagined the thunder of hooves.

"I believe," she said rising to her feet, "that I'll say goodnight. It's been a long day and I want to feel rested tomorrow."

Her grandfather and Mrs. Hazelton both rose and walked her to the door. "Breakfast will be about 8 o'clock, Jamie," Mrs. Hazelton said. "But if you oversleep, don't worry. Things operate on a flexible schedule here."

As Jamie ascended the stairs she noted, subconsciously, that it was the fourth step from the bottom that squeaked.

Her room was attractively furnished, Jamie realized. A large brass bed stood against the north wall and the chest of drawers and the dresser were solid oak as was the long and heavy wardrobe. The carpet, a rich dark wine color, felt delightfully soft as she slipped off her shoes and ran her feet across the deep pile.

Sometime in the last twenty years, Jamie thought, the cattle business must have smiled on John Bowie Ballantine; everything in the house appeared tasteful and expensive. Yet her grandfather had spoken of the "hard times" of the nineties and Jamie knew from her own experiences that those had been difficult years.

Perhaps he had some source of income he did not choose to discuss. But this seemed unlikely and she dismissed the possibility.

The lamp that Annie had lighted earlier stood on the dresser and reflected in the polished brass knobs of the bed, touching the corners of the room gently. How much softer than the garish electric bulbs in her Missouri home! Electricity would be a long time coming to Bien Escondido and the better for it, she thought.

A small writing table stood underneath the east window of the room and she decided to bring her diary up to date. She had no entries since leaving Missouri except for brief comments on her train experiences. She removed the diary from her luggage, sat down at the table and began to write:

> *May 14, 1912. Bien Escondido.*
>
> *Arrived here this afternoon safe but very tired. The ranch house is pleasant and my room delightful. I cannot say as much for the land; it becomes most forbidding a hundred yards away from the ranch house and the little lake. Not only forbidding, but downright dangerous. It must surely be filled with rattlesnakes, scorpions and other unpleasant creatures. Otherwise, it is – empty. There aren't even many cattle. Grandpa says the rancher who leases this land got caught short last year and had to sell off most of his herd.*
>
> *I can look out the east window of my room just above the writing desk and see Castle Gap. Or at least I could if it were not dark now. Something about it fascinates me. Yes, frightens me a little, I know not why. I have only a vague feeling that there is some sort of danger or some evil thing out there. Something out of history that got stuck in time, somehow, and is still waiting to happen.*
>
> *Foolishness, of course.*
>
> *We are to have a young man as a summer guest, I understand. He is coming in two weeks. I hope his appear-*

ance will liven things up some, since otherwise the prospect would be for a long and dull summer, I'm afraid.

Mrs. Hazelton seems pleasant enough although somewhat reserved. Possibly that is just her nature. She doesn't make me feel unwelcome – just not overly welcome. Perhaps she fears that I will somehow try to take her position in the household which would be the last thing in my mind.

Dr. Black will be coming out to the ranch tomorrow, they tell me, and will stay for a while. He sounds like an interesting man. Grandfather says he is full of stories about the old days. At least he will be someone different to talk to.

Mrs. Hazelton says that I am to call her "Ruth." It will not be easy. She must be thirty years older than I. But...I'll try. Starting tomorrow.

Jamie closed the diary and fastened the small brass hasp. Where to keep it, she wondered. Certainly not out in plain sight for there would surely be times when she would want to record some very personal thoughts. She finally decided on a snap-down compartment in the larger of her two suitcases. It held the diary neatly and anyone looking in the suitcase would assume it to be empty.

The brass bed proved to be wonderfully comfortable and she drifted quickly into sleep.

CHAPTER 3

Jamie found herself in the middle of a rutted road that wound through mesquite and cactus and up a gentle slope toward a low pass between two hills or mesas. It was twilight. Instinctively, she knew she was on the road that led through Castle Cap. Behind her was the solid security of her grandfather's house which she left only minutes before but, upon looking back, she could see nothing.

She pressed forward up the road not knowing why, certain with each step that she should turn and run but was unable to do so. The white objects along the road had first appeared to be rocks, now had become the bleached skulls of horses or cows. It was a road down which most certainly high adventure and stark tragedy had ridden hand-in-hand. Somewhere ahead she knew there lay waiting some evil, dangerous force, a thing from which she should flee but to which she was inexorably drawn.

She became aware of a distant sound that came from the pass ahead. The sound grew quickly in intensity, first to a low rumble then to a heavier drumbeat. It seemed to rise and fall, each tumultuous wave larger than the last. Suddenly there erupted from the crest in front of her a twisting, tumbling, tortured mass, black and evil, thrusting itself irresistibly upon her. Buffalo! Thousands of them, driven by the madness of thirst toward the distant river.

She looked frantically to each side for anything that might offer protection. Nothing. And so she turned and ran, hopelessly, on leaden feet, propelled by legs that rose and fell with agonizing slowness. The thunder of hooves suddenly reached a crashing crescendo and, turning her head, she saw that the fearful wave was only yards away.

"Oh God! Help me, help me!" she heard herself scream.

Instantly there was total silence, broken a moment later by the scratching of a match. Annie lighted the lamp. Jamie was sitting bolt-upright in her bed, heart pounding violently, cold perspiration on her brow. A brilliant flash of lightning momentarily washed out the yellow glow of the lamp and a heavy roll of thunder followed. Weakly, she realized that a summer thunderstorm had provided the sound effects for her nightmare of stampeding buffalo.

"Miss Jamie, you were crying for help! Are you all right?" Annie asked, anxiety creasing her brow.

"I guess so," Jamie replied. "Yes. Yes, of course, it was just a bad dream, a truly bad one."

Annie came over to the bed and gave her a reassuring pat on the shoulder. "I always say, the nice thing about bad dreams is when you wake up and find out they ain't so. Lots better than having a good dream and then finding out none of it is going to come true. Best thing is no dreams at all, I reckon."

Well, Jamie thought as Annie closed the door, she might be right. No dreams at all. But what would life be, she wondered, without dreams. Dull and unimaginative, doubtless. For, didn't the night time dream hold an uncertain mirror to the daytime thought? Had she not read somewhere that dreams were of considerable significance in psychological analysis? If that were so, then what was the meaning of the frightful terror of the buffalo stampede?

Still pondering this question, she fell asleep.

CHAPTER 4

The thunderstorm had brought a considerable rain, cooling and freshening the morning air. Fragments of snow-white clouds were racing across the sky in a belated attempt to catch up with the thunderheads which still rose majestically in the distant east. Like chicks scurrying to find a misplaced mother hen, Jamie thought.

"Better enjoy the air while you can, Jamie," her grandfather said. "It'll be hot again before noon."

Across the breakfast table, Mrs. Hazelton nodded agreement.

"You'll get used to the climate in a week or so," she said. "A month at most. If not by then, probably never. Some folks have to give up on it." There was a good chance she would fall into the latter category, Jamie thought and was about to say so but changed the subject instead.

"I suppose you heard all the commotion I caused last night. I'm sorry if anyone was disturbed but the thing was so terribly real. It seems foolish this morning but I was scared half to death last night." She described the dream as best she could remember.

"Maybe it would help if we went over to the Gap this morning," her grandfather suggested, "so that you can see there's nothing stronger than imagination out there."

"If it's all right with you, grandpa, I'd rather not. This morning is still too close to last night. Maybe in three or four days. Let me get familiar with the area around the ranch house today."

Jamie's tour of Bien Escondido began with a walk around the house. "This is what we call a Texas lawn," her grandfather said pointing out the neatly raked gravel and decorative groupings of colorful rocks. "There isn't any grass, of course, but no weeds, either. And now you know the real reason why I keep on living here. I never did like mowing a lawn."

At the rear of the house was another carefully tended area and, surprisingly, a small rock garden with cactus and some blooming plants that she could not identify. One of the two windmills stood behind the house and next to it an elevated water tank.

"This well supplies the house," her grandfather said. "The tank holds five hundred gallons. Made out of redwood all the way from California. The windmill operates a force pump which fills the tank with water that then runs by gravity down to the house. Only inside plumbing for thirty-five miles." He was obviously pleased with these technical accomplishments, Jamie saw.

"The other windmill and water tank down there supply the bunkhouse and the corral which is almost never used anymore, and irrigate Ruth's vegetable and flower gardens. She will probably want to show off what we can raise here if we have water. Without the wells, we could not exist."

The next stop was the lake, some two hundred yards from the ranch house down a gentle slope. It was roughly oval in shape, about two hundred yards wide and slightly greater in length. Marshy grass grew around its edge and a few small trees.

"It seems a little unreal," Jamie said. "In such a dry area. Are there underground springs?"

"Not that I know of," her grandfather replied. "The lake is fed by an arroyo which comes in from the northeast and goes right up into Castle Gap. It's bone dry normally, but when we occasionally get a really heavy rain, an astonishingly lot of water comes down. It drains all the west side of the Castle Mountain area. The lake is a natural low spot and traps all the water that comes down. Of course, when we have a long dry spell, the level of the lake drops a lot but the next big downpour fills it up again. I've never seen it dry."

They walked along the west side of the lake to the arroyo. Although the previous night's storm had not produced a lot of rain, a thin trickle of water ran down the arroyo and into the lake.

"Grandpa, why couldn't you have built the ranch house right next to the lake? It would have been such a pretty setting for it. Cooler, too, maybe." Jamie hastened to add, "Not that it isn't nice enough now, of course."

"A logical question and it has a logical answer. Two of them, in fact. First, we were planning to start up a cattle ranch. The lake, which is not salty or alkaline, was an obvious watering place for range cattle. You know how it is with cows. They don't come for water one at a time but all seem to get the urge simultaneously. Who would want them parading through the ranch house yard, trampling the flowers, knocking things down? It just wouldn't have worked.

"The second reason was the wells. I had to be sure of a good well before I started on the house and other buildings. So I brought in an old fellow from east of Goodland – only name I ever heard for him was Manuel – who had a big reputation for witching water wells. His wand didn't show much near the lake shore, but just went crazy over where you see the wells now. I've been a believer ever since.''

They returned to the house and Jamie sought the comfort of the shaded porch; it was, as her grandfather predicted, going to be hot before noon. Mrs. Hazelton came out in a few moments.

''What are your plans for this fall, Jamie?'' she asked. ''Do you think a teaching position is still in the picture?''

''Possibly but I would have to say in honesty not probably. I applied to ten schools. Four of them had already filled the vacancy. Three others required qualification in secondary courses that I did not have. Two said that my qualifications were satisfactory and that I would hear from them soon. They have my address in care of grandfather's box number in Goodland. The tenth school didn't acknowledge my application at all.''

Mrs. Hazelton considered this for a few moments before replying and then appeared to weigh her second question carefully. ''Please don't regard me as presumptuous, Jamie, or overly inquisitive, but your future concerns me, now more than ever. Don't answer this if you'd rather not, but isn't there someone back home – in Missouri, I mean – who may have a special place in your life?''

It's a little much, Jamie thought. *The very first day!* She had been looking out into the yard where a small lizard was scurrying from one rock pile to another but she leveled her gaze now on Mrs. Hazelton.

''I have,'' she said in a voice which she hoped was not impolite but still appropriately cool, ''a number of close friends. Some of them are young men. I presume that's what you were referring to. I'm in no hurry to rush back to any one of them.''

It was not the answer Mrs. Hazelton desired. The woman's face was transparent, Jamie saw, and this realization gave her a tiny taste of victory. Ruth Hazelton's inability to conceal feelings might be useful should an adversary relationship develop. Somehow, Jamie thought uneasily, this could be a possibility.

With what appeared to be a definite effort, Mrs. Hazelton changed the subject. ''Dr. Black ought to be showing up here this afternoon,'' she said. ''I'm sure you'll find him most interesting. He's been away for a few days to San Antonio, I think. He goes there occasionally.''

''They must be what one would call 'cronies,' '' Jamie said.

''More than that. He's been your grandfather's dear and closest friend for nearly thirty years I'd guess, and they're almost like brothers. Ever since your grandmother passed away eight years ago, he's come out to the ranch to look after things whenever John leaves on a business trip or for any other reason. He came out and stayed while your grandfather was in Missouri last month. Believe me, it gives us a sense of security to have him here while John is away."

"Why," she continued, "he even comes out to keep an eye on things when we go in to town. John takes us once a week to get things and to visit friends. Annie usually goes along so there wouldn't be anyone here at all for most of the day, if it weren't for Morgan Black."

"What does he do out here, Ruth, when he's alone?"

"He fishes occasionally. We can usually count on his catching enough for supper. He also reads, we have a good library. John takes several magazines, too.

"And he plays solitaire for hours at a time. Keeps a record of his 'losses' and his 'winnings.' The last I heard he said he was ahead about $600. He keeps joking about 'paying himself' and starting over. When both of them are here, they play dominoes and talk about politics and cattle prices."

Dominoes, politics and prices. How could she fit into such conversations, Jamie wondered and began to wish that young Mr. Thatcher's school would hurry up and end so he could come on out to the ranch.

He'll be scholarly, no doubt. Who else would spend a summer looking for evidence of pre-Indian culture in a social desert? Tall, but gangling, clumsy. He'll be nearsighted and wear thick glasses and speak knowledgeably about the classics of literature.

These thoughts were not encouraging and she began to explore alternatives. A young instructor in a small college would have a master's degree. He would probably be working toward a doctorate. Why, of course! The summer expedition in Bien Escondido would eventually find its way into a doctoral dissertation. Perhaps it would be done brilliantly and lead to immediate promotion to full professor and then to head of the department. Maybe even to a chancellor's chair at some university, in time!

Suddenly Mr. Thatcher seemed more interesting. A man of medium build, handsome in a definitely masculine way, with blond hair that had a slight tendency to wave. The glasses disappeared, replaced by a boyish smile. Jamie smiled back in return.

Mrs. Hazelton rose, announcing that she needed to confer with Annie about routine details, and returned to the house. If she noticed Jamie's smile, she made no comment.

Early in the afternoon, on her grandfather's suggestion, Jamie was given a tour of the flower and vegetable gardens. Somewhere between the tomatoes and the sweet corn they heard an approaching car.

Jamie's first impression of Morgan Black was favorable. Although approximately the same age as her grandfather, the resemblance ceased there. John Bowie Ballantine was the complete western man, from high-heeled boots to Stetson. Dr. Morgan Black could have just stepped from his office in Fort Worth or San Antonio.

He looked, Jamie thought, like anything but a small-town doctor. *Why he probably doesn't even have a little black bag in his car.* And his clothing had most certainly not come from a mail-order catalog.

"It's so nice to meet you," Dr. Black was saying. "Your granddaddy has told me all about you and I've been looking forward to your coming. Believe me, it will be a relief to have someone with a few fresh ideas to talk to. I've heard all of John's jokes forty times over and he's heard mine. On top of that, he gets so excited over the Teddy Roosevelt versus Taft affair that he can't concentrate on dominoes. Takes all the fun out of winning."

"And just how often have you been winning lately?" Mr. Ballantine said. "I seem to remember you lost about four dollars in our last session. And speaking of politics, that Roosevelt-Taft thing is going to let us Democrats into the White House this fall, take my word on it."

"I'm afraid I can't contribute much to a political discussion," Jamie said. "I know there's something about mugwumps but I don't know what one is, really, just that it doesn't sound very flattering. If you don't mind, Dr. Black, rather than discussing something I know little or nothing about, I'd like to have you show me your new car. That I understand."

Be sure to ask him about his car. It's new and the biggest thing in his life, Mrs. Hazelton had said on the way from the gardens to the house.

Dr. Black hastened to comply. "It's the only Packard in the county," he said, beaming, "and they tell me it will do seventy miles an hour. No place around here to drive like that, of course, unless you took it to some fairgrounds race track and even then it probably wouldn't hold the corners."

"It's beautiful," Jamie said. "You must take me for a ride in it. Not today, but soon." She glanced covertly at Mrs. Hazelton and received an almost imperceptible nod of approval.

They returned to the living room and fell into an exchange of small talk. Jamie once more related her experiences in coming from Missouri and Morgan Black contributed an account of his latest trip to San Antonio.

About 4 o'clock, Mr. Ballantine and Dr. Black asked to be excused for a time and went down the path to the edge of the lake. There they seemed to be engaged in a serious conversation Jamie could see from the window, although they were too far away to be heard.

Politics, prices or dominoes. Probably the first, Jamie decided.

CHAPTER 5

"Keep your voice down, John. I think we're too far away for anyone to hear, but there's no sense in taking chances."

"Well, speak your piece," Ballantine replied.

"I think you know what I'm going to say, John. We've been over this ground before and I thought we were in agreement. We've been lucky so far and, for whatever reason, the arrangement has worked. No one has known except the two of us and your wife, who has been gone for eight years now.

"When you brought Ruth Hazelton out as housekeeper, I couldn't object too much. S'pose I would have done the same thing myself. But dammit, John, the woman has a suspicious nature. Sometimes I can see the questions in her mind. One of these days, she's going to ask them."

"But that's not what's bothering you, is it Morgan? What's in your craw is my granddaughter in the house for the summer."

"That, on top of your young college professor friend," Black replied. "It was bad enough giving him permission to prowl around the ranch for a couple of months without putting somebody right in the house. We've had it pretty well worked out to get Ruth into town every week or so to shop, and Annie to go along at the same time to visit her sister. Miss Jamie is another matter and getting all three of them out of the house at the same time won't be easy. And even then, there's your young friend Thatcher knocking around the place too close for comfort. I tell you, John, I just don't like it."

"I'm sorry, Morgan," Ballantine replied. "I really don't see it as a threat. My granddaughter will respect the privacy of my den. I keep it locked and carry the only key. Thatcher will be living in the foreman's room at the bunkhouse and will be in the main house only by invitation when the rest of us are there."

"I guess it's Thatcher who bothers me most of all," Black replied. "I have never been able to buy that story about pre-Indian culture. I have a very uneasy feeling that the man has gotten wind of something, somehow. Maybe some leak in our San Antonio connection, although I've been extremely careful about that. He may even be a private investigator retained by the Mexican government."

Ballantine didn't reply for a few moments during which time he lighted a cigar, carefully inspecting the ascending smoke.

"Could that be a possibility," he said, "after all these years?"

"Yes, indeed," Black replied. "We're talking about a very large sum of money or its equivalent and even more, national pride. Mexicans are long on that, you know. I think they would make an effort at recovery if they were sure. After all, the question of our legitimate ownership was the original and basic reason for everything we've done for the last twenty-four years. I think the matter is just as relevant now as it was in 1888."

"How much do you reckon there is left?" Ballantine asked.

"More than half of it. Only a guess, but fairly close I think."

Ballantine nodded in agreement. Then he studied the distant horizon a minute before replying.

"Morgan, I've never really given this serious consideration until now. Never seemed any reason to. But you realize that at the present rate it'll be close to twenty-five years before we clean it all out. That would be somewhere around 1935. I'll be ninety-five years old and you are a year or two older. The time has come to bring this thing to a conclusion, somehow."

"I agree, John. But I suggest we play it close to the vest this summer. I think we should lie low and make no move whatever until September. By then Mr. Thatcher will have returned to his duties and, if he is conducting an investigation for anybody, will send in a negative report. And Jamie will have gone back to Missouri."

"Speaking of my granddaughter, Morgan," Ballantine said, "You know she's all I have. When my son and his wife died so tragically last month, Jamie became my only heir. Whatever I have when my time comes goes to her and I want everything clean and proper, with a will and all. That means you and I have to complete the conversion to cash and each take our share."

"Probably none of my business, John , but we've been in this thing so long and know each other so well, I think I can speak freely. What about Ruth Hazelton?"

"Well, what about her?" Ballantine asked.

"Just this. Maybe you haven't noticed, but I have. It seems in the

24

last couple of years, she considers herself something more than your housekeeper. Your..common-law wife. If she believes she has that status, she may expect to be remembered in your will. I'm not sure about the legal aspects, but she may be able to inherit from you, will or no will.

"And another thing. I feel she probably knows enough about your circumstances to realize you have some source of income other than the ranch. This must puzzle her and I expect her to begin asking questions, and soon. Your granddaughter's arrival on the scene can have no other effect than to heighten anxiety about her own security in the event of your death."

Ballantine, in deep concentration, had permitted his cigar to go out. He lighted it and turned to Black.

"Some of these matters I've given thought to from time to time recently. Others had not occurred to me and I thank you for calling my attention to them. I have no will at present. What would you suggest?"

" I wouldn't wait, John. Take the train to Ft. Worth in the next few days and consult an attorney there. I believe that would be preferable to retaining someone in this county. The less people around here know about things the better. You could tell Ruth and Jamie that your trip is in connection with possible lease revisions. If you want to tell them about the provisions of your will after you've executed it, you can decide then.

"One more thing," Black continued. "Don't mention in your will any specific property other than the ranch. If we can get everything converted into cash and divided between us later this fall, you could set up a trust fund of some sort for Jamie with whatever part of the cash you wanted to give her and let the remaining money and the ranch land be distributed under your will. The attorneys will know how to take care of the details. And they don't need to know the source of the funds."

"I think you're right, Morgan," Ballantine said. "I'll go in to Ft. Worth in the next few days. The trust fund for Jamie is a good idea and I'll discuss it with the attorney in addition to having the will drawn. It wouldn't be possible to actually set up the trust, of course, until the cash is available. Right now we don't even know how much it will amount to."

Ballantine turned and started toward the house.

"Wait up a bit, John," Black said. "There's something more that has to be said and now's the time for it. I've been completely honest with you in all details connected with our gentlemen's agreement. You know everything there is about me. Except for one thing. I have a son."

Ballantine stared for a moment in disbelief. "But you told me you were never married, Morgan. You said you planned to be but that your fiancee died, years before I knew you. From scarlet fever."

"Only partly true. We were never married and she did die. But not from fever. My Melanie died in childbirth. Our son lived. Melanie's parents were furious when they discovered her condition. They were determined that I would never see Melanie again or our child. She was sent to live with an aunt in Ohio and a story was made up that she was widowed, that her husband had lost his life in the war. This was summer, 1864. My son was born and Melanie died in March 1865, just past her eighteenth birthday."

"Hold up now, Morgan," Ballantine interrupted. "You don't have to tell me these personal details. I'm not sure I want you to. Anyway, it was more than forty years ago."

"I think you should know, John. They've been bottled up inside me too long. Some you already know. That I was a medical student and planned to join the army of the Confederacy when those studies were completed. And that I served as a medical officer the last few months of the war.

"When Melanie's parents sent her away, I had already joined General Beauregard's command and, although I requested leave of absence, it was denied. One letter came from Melanie. She had it smuggled out somehow. I was frantic to get back but the situation for the Confederacy was deteriorating so rapidly by early 1865 that there was no chance.

"After things finally fell apart in April, I was able to start back to our home in Kentucky and arrived in May. It was only then that I learned of Melanie's death and that I was the father of a son.

"Melanie's father held me responsible for his daughter's death and swore that I would never see my son. The aunt, a widow, moved several times taking the baby with her and, as I learned later, changed her name and my son's at least twice.

"I had no funds to pursue a search, but did the best I could for several months. You can imagine how much cooperation I got in Ohio and Indiana ...I was an officer in the Confederate army, a rebel who had helped those who were killing their husbands and brothers. Doors were shut everywhere.

"Finally, I had to give up. My father and mother had moved to Texas in September 1865. It seemed like a good idea to leave Kentucky and start a new life somewhere else. I hung out my shingle in eastern Kansas for a few years, then in 1870 joined my parents in Denton, Texas. My father had a good medical practice by that time and there was a future for me there."

"All of which," Ballantine said thoughtfully, "has to have a bearing on our present situation and relationship. I assume you located your son."

"Yes, John, I did. But not until a few years ago. In 1904, actually. You may recall that in the summer of 1903 I made a special trip to St. Louis. I can't remember now what reason I gave for going. I recall that you made some joking remarks about my returning with a wife and offered all sorts of advice about avoiding entrapment.

"I hired the Pinkerton organization there to make an exhaustive search for my son. I had sufficient funds by then and the expense didn't matter. I gave them all the information I had, although it was old and offered no more than a place to start. An experienced man gave his time to my case exclusively. The search led through four states and about a dozen communities before it was successfully concluded. Pinkerton's fees and travel expenses came to more than $10,000, but I never regretted a penny of it."

"Where is he now?"

"They located him in a small town in eastern Nebraska. Still lives there, married, has two children. He's a partner in a real estate and insurance business and is doing well. The aunt died years ago. The Pinkerton man, posing as a possible purchaser of farm land, had several conversations with my son and learned about as much as he could without arousing suspicion. The aunt had given him the name of Charles Jackson, the surname coming from her family. He was forty-seven last March."

"And he doesn't know?" Ballantine asked. "He still thinks his father was killed in the Civil War?"

"That's right. I've thought about it a thousand times, wondering what to do. No question that it would be traumatic for him and for his wife and children if I showed up and tore apart everything that he believed about his life. At the same time I'm desperate to know him, to know my grandchildren, to feel that someone will be carrying on after I'm gone."

"You've thrown a lot at me in a pretty short time, Morgan," Ballantine said. "Don't know if I can digest it in one afternoon. Or give you very good advice. All I know is what I would do if it were my decision. Maybe you don't want to hear it. You haven't asked."

"I'm asking now, John. What would you do?"

"The only thing that makes sense. Your son has believed himself to be an orphan from the time of his birth. No brothers or sisters, no family except the one he has created. I know nothing of his circumstances but from what you have said, they must be modest.

"Think what you would be in a position to do. Your son could expand his business or move to a larger community. Your grandchildren would be able to pursue advanced college educations and have other advantages their parents did not enjoy. And you would have your own family at last, and not the distant shadow of one, which is all you have now."

"You're forgetting one thing, John...that Melanie and I were never married. How long do you think it would take for him to realize what that fact makes him?"

"Not necessary, Morgan. You could tell him that you and Melanie were married secretly and that the records were lost in a fire. And that Melanie's parents sent her away because they were bitterly opposed to you for religious reasons. Or because they were Union sympathizers and you a Confederate officer. Lord, there are a dozen plausible stories., And who is going to be able to prove you wrong after all these years?"

"I'll think on it, John. I want desperately to claim my family but I don't want to hurt them in the process. I appreciate your suggestions. I think they're good and I may decide to follow them. I'll get my thinking pulled together by the time you get back from Ft. Worth."

They turned toward the house, now, moving slowly up the path, each lost in private thoughts.

Jamie, who had returned to the porch, watched their approach and she thought whatever they had been discussing would remained an unresolved problem. The Taft-Roosevelt thing, probably.

CHAPTER 6

The next few days passed quietly at Bien Escondido. Jamie busied herself about the house, spending time weeding and tending the garden and in browsing through her grandfather's extensive library. Ruth had been working on a quilt off and on for the last year and she enlisted Jamie's help for most of one afternoon. Her grandfather had embarked on a project to rebuild the sign at the ranch entry gate.

About the middle of the week he announced, however, that it was time to take Jamie to Castle Gap to allay her apprehension about the place.

It was nearly three miles to the top of the Gap and they could go about half of that distance by car. The road, which followed the old stage trail in places, was a poor one at best and had been damaged by a severe storm the previous fall. They could drive by car, he said, to the first washout and then walk the rest of the way.

"I know it's stupid and childish," Jamie said as they began the walk from the car, "to be fearful of something as innocent as a piece of landscape. I can't explain it. The feeling was there suddenly and strongly the very first day and before the nightmare about it. The place just seemed to contain a hidden danger."

"Nothing up there to be afraid of, Jamie, other than maybe an occasional rattlesnake and they're inactive in the heat of day."

Near the summit, Ballantine halted beside a rocky outcrop to the left of the trail. It was the spot where desperadoes had held up an eastbound stage he said. The old trail made a sharp turn here and, going uphill, the stage was slowed to a walk. The bandits had hidden behind the rocky outcrop and had stepped out in front of the horses.

"According to legend," Ballantine continued, "they got away with a gold shipment worth about $10,000 and the personal effects of the passengers. The holdup men were run down a few days later while attempting to cross into Mexico and one of them was shot. The loot was never recovered."

Jamie closed her eyes and the scene leaped into vivid focus. She was, for a brief moment, one of the stage passengers returning fearlessly the cold and evil stares of the bandits.

"I have nothing," she said in a firm voice hoping they would not notice the tiny gold locket at her neck.

"How's that?" she heard her grandfather ask and realized that she had spoken aloud. "Nothing, grandpa," she said, embarrassed. "Just an over-active imagination."

At the top of the pass they paused to rest a few moments, to survey the empty plain to the east and then to the west the old trail that had led so many years ago to the distant Pecos and the Horsehead Crossing.

It was true, she thought. There was nothing to be afraid of. The sun-bleached animal skulls so prominent in her dream were nowhere to be seen. The last stage had passed through two generations ago along with the last bandit. Stampeding buffalo, if they ever existed, could be recalled by only the oldest of persons.

On the way back to the ranch, Ballantine pointed to a spot a few hundred yards from the end of the lake where, he said, it was believed Indians had attacked several freight wagons sometime in the 1860s. Little or nothing was known about this event, he explained, since there had been no survivors. The Indians burned the wagons and the only thing remaining had been the rusted wagon irons at the location. These were still visible as late as 1890, Ballantine said, but no trace remained now.

After supper that evening while they were still seated at the table, Ballantine made the announcement.

"I've decided to go to Fort Worth for a few days. I plan to leave on the 25th. The ranch is leased as three separate tracts with the exception of about a hundred acres that includes the ranch house area. Two of the leases expire at the end of the year and the other one runs out next March 1. The leases are silent as to mineral rights and this has bothered me. I want to clarify that I retain all mineral rights and the right of access for mineral exploration at all times. I realize the leases have several months to run yet, but if some negotiation is necessary, I want to allow plenty of time."

"Couldn't you handle this by correspondence?" Ruth asked.

"I've considered it but I'd feel a lot more comfortable sitting down with them and hashing out the details. I know next to nothing about retention of mineral rights. And anyway, I've got a small shopping list. Headed by a new pair of boots."

"Will you be back by the 28th?" Ruth asked. "That's the date the young archaeologist arrives. Thatcher said he would be coming in on the afternoon train — that's the same one you were on, Jamie."

"It is possible that I may be able to come back on the same train, although I think the 29th would be more likely. Morgan understands the arrangements and will plan to stay at the ranch while I'm gone. He can drive you to Goodland to pick up Mr. Thatcher. If I'm on the same train, fine. If not, plan to meet the train again the next day."

"All right, John," Ruth said. "And I'm sure you won't mind adding a few items to your Fort Worth shopping list. Mostly for the house. One or two personal things for me. And speaking of shopping, I suppose we're going in to Goodland Saturday morning?"

"Yes, about 9 o'clock, if that's agreeable to everybody. Morgan will come out about that time and we can leave as soon as he gets here. He's wandering around outside right now but I think he plans to stay overnight and go back sometime Sunday."

Saturday morning was pleasantly cool which would make the trip to town more agreeable, Jamie thought. Dr. Black arrived on schedule and the weekly shopping expedition got underway. Ballantine asked Jamie to sit with him in the front seat "so I can point out anything of interest we might have missed coming out to the ranch." Ruth and Annie took the rear seat.

Ballantine stopped for a moment at the entrance gate to permit proper admiration of his carpentry and painting efforts on the new sign.

"It's a true work of art, grandpa," Jamie said. "If the ranching business falls on hard times you can always go into the sign painting game." Annie added her approval, Ruth remained silent.

The woman is annoyed by the back seat arrangement, Jamie thought. *She probably thinks her rightful position has been taken by a newcomer.*

Although Ruth's displeasure seemed obvious to Jamie, her grandfather did not notice, or at least gave no indication. He rattled off a string of comments on everything from the condition of the range to the political unrest across the river in Mexico.

The first stop was the home of Annie's sister, a small frame house in the east part of Goodland, where Annie was warmly received by an assortment of ragged but happy children.

"Expect us back to pick you up somewhere around 2 o'clock," Ballantine called to her as they drove away.

"I'm going to let you and Jamie out at MacPherson's store, Ruth," he said, "and then drive over to Johnson's garage. He expected a shipment of new tires this week and I want to make a deal for a couple, if I like what I see." Ruth and Jamie stepped out of the car into the dusty street across from the store.

ANDREW MACPHERSON — GENERAL MERCHANDISE the sign proclaimed in bold lettering above the fashionable, curved metal awning. It was, Jamie noted, the only metal awning in the block. The others were canvas in various stages of disrepair, flapping in the morning breeze. On the glass door, the customer was advised: "If MacPherson doesn't have it, you don't need it."

There were two clerks in the store but Mr. MacPherson came out immediately from his small office to wait on Ruth Hazelton personally. After introducing Jamie, Ruth handed MacPherson her shopping list.

"Might as well put you to work, Jamie," she said. "I want to go over to Virginia's for a while. My dressmaker, Virginia Dolan. Her place is just around the corner from the end of the block. She has been working on a couple of things for me. You take care of the list and, mind you, don't let Andrew give you anything but top quality."

"Oh, we'll get along fine, Ruth. He reminds me of our preacher back home and I'm sure he's honest."

Filling Ruth's order took only fifteen or twenty minutes.

"No place to wait out there," MacPherson said, "except for the loafer's bench over by the stove. Might as well make yourself comfortable in my office. If I know Ruth Hazelton, it'll be a while. If John had a telephone out at the ranch, it wouldn't take Ruth so long to catch up on the town gossip."

A leather-covered chair across from MacPherson's desk looked inviting and Jamie settled herself comfortably in it.

"I've been looking forward to the opportunity of meeting you, Miss Ballantine," MacPherson said, "ever since John told me a couple of weeks ago that you would be coming. We have something in common. As a boy, I lived less than ten miles from your town and, although I left Missouri more than twenty years ago, I'm sure there must be families living there now whom we both know. I still have some shirt-tail relatives, second cousins and the like, in the area."

MacPherson named six or eight families, several of whom were familiar to Jamie and she supplied current details.

"You said you came to Goodland more than twenty years ago, Mr. MacPherson. Was that about the same time grandfather came?"

'I beat him by a year or so, Miss Ballantine. I came in the spring of '88 and he showed up in the summer of 1889. I know he bought land west of Castle Gap in the fall of that year and then in 1890 built Bien Escondido. I have never been able to figure out why."

"He says he was moved by the spirit of adventure, Mr. MacPherson. The land was cheap and he thought there was a good chance it would appreciate in value. What brought you out? You're considerably younger than grandpa. Was it adventure and excitement?"

"More accurate to say the need to eat three square meals a day, Miss Jamie. I was a surveyor and out of work and when a chance came to get on the railroad survey crew working in this area, I took it. Stayed with the railroad a couple of years and then two of us started this general store. I bought out my partner ten years ago."

Jamie thought a moment. "When did you come here as a railroad surveyor, Mr. MacPherson?"

"In 1888. March, I think."

"And the railroad was committed to its present location, where the tracks are now, at that time?"

"Oh, yes, indeed," MacPherson replied. "They decided the route the previous fall and began acquiring right-of-way early in 1888. That's where the survey crew came in. Are you interested in the early history of the area, Miss Jamie?"

"I'm mostly curious about how things were when grandpa came out. There has been a lot of progress since then, I'm sure."

She arose, suddenly feeling confused. She needed a few quiet moments to pull her thinking together.

"Mr. MacPherson, I've enjoyed our visit but I mustn't take any more of your time. I'll go around the corner and find that dressmaker's place. Surely Ruth must be about finished by now. We can pick up our purchases this afternoon if that's all right."

"They'll be just inside the door. You won't have any trouble finding Mrs. Dolan's shop. Turn left at the corner and it's the third door."

Ruth and Jamie met at the corner. "We'll just walk on over to the Texan Hotel," Ruth said. "It's almost 12 and I planned to meet John at the dining room at noon. They usually serve a good meal there."

The hotel dining room was clean and attractive with red and white checkered tablecloths and a menu that surprised Jamie by its extent and variety. Ballantine had stopped at the post office on his way back from Johnson's garage and handed Jamie two letters.

"Go ahead and read them here if you wish, Jamie," her grandfather said.

One letter was from her attorney who reported that he had received the proceeds of the life insurance policy and had deposited them to her account in the local bank pending further instructions. The other letter was from the school that had not yet replied to her teaching application. There was no vacancy in the fall term.

A letter had also come to Mr. Ballantine from Dick Thatcher. He would arrive a day earlier than planned, on the 27th.

"So there won't be any chance that we'll be on the same train," Ballantine said. "You folks and Doc Black will have to do the welcoming honors. I'll definitely plan to come on the 29th."

The drive back to the ranch after picking up Annie and the purchases at MacPherson's store, was uneventful except for Ballantine's announcement that he might consider buying a new-fangled home electric plant. They weren't available yet, Ballantine said, but Johnson's Garage expected to get the agency in the fall and set up a demonstration unit before the end of the year. They operated with a small generator driven by a gasoline engine and storage batteries.

Jamie remembered her earlier assessment that electricity would be a long time coming to Bien Escondido. She'd have to change her mind about that, it appeared.

After supper, Ballantine and Dr. Black retired to the library and began the usual evening of dominoes. Ruth settled herself at the dining room table after the dishes were removed and began to scan several Fort Worth newspapers they had brought from town.

"If you don't mind, Ruth, I think I'll go up to my room and lie down for a while," Jamie said. "I might write a few letters to friends and to my attorney. Dr. Black can mail them Monday, if it isn't too much trouble."

"He won't mind at all, Jamie," Ruth replied. "And you go right ahead with your letter writing. I've got plenty to keep me occupied down here."

After lighting the lamp in her room, Jamie sat by the writing desk for several minutes staring out into the gathering darkness. The vague, unexplained feeling of uneasiness which had troubled her from the day of her arrival suddenly became much more intense.

To sort out her jumbled thoughts, she determined to write them down. Had it not always eased her mind, somehow, to confide in her diary? She brought it from its hiding place, noting that there had been no entries for several days.

CHAPTER 7

May 22, 1912

I have been at Bien Escondido for a little more than a week. It seemed at first that it might be a dull summer and I gave thought to cutting my visit short and returning to Missouri after three weeks or so. Not now, though. There is something going on here that I do not understand, a mystery that defies solution. I may be, probably am, asking for trouble, but I am going to have a try at finding out what is going on.

Somehow, it involves grandfather Ballantine. Dr. Black is mixed up in it too. From what they have told me plus what I have observed, they make very certain that one of them is at the ranch at all times. If grandpa has to go away for a while, even for only a few hours, the Doctor has to rush right out and stay while he is gone. They say it is just to be helpful, to "keep an eye on things." Maybe so, but what things!

The thought occurred to me that there was something between Dr. Black and Ruth Hazelton but I doubt it. In the first place it is too obvious. And I am sure Ruth would not risk endangering what she believes is a very good arrangement, one that might be highly rewarding when grandpa is gone.

Today something happened that confuses me although I am certain that it has some sort of part in the whole picture. A week ago I asked grandfather how he happened to select the location of Bien Escondido near the old trail leading out of Castle Gap. He said he thought the soon-to-be-built railroad might come through Castle Gap, traverse his ranch and thereby make it far more valuable. This was, he said, in the fall of 1889 and he put up the ranch buildings in 1890.

At MacPherson's store in Goodland this morning, Mr. MacPherson told me that he had worked as a surveyor for the railroad in 1888 more than a year before grandfather came out and that it was common knowledge that the railroad would be located where it is now, far to the north of Castle Gap. Mr. MacPherson also recalled that he came to the area a year before grandfather.

It distresses me to say, but it seems that grandfather's explanation for Bien Escondido's location was fabricated. Why! Why would he deceive me! The only answer seems to be that the true explanation must require concealment.

Now that I think of it, I'm beginning to wonder about the very name of this place. Bien Escondido, indeed! One would have to try very hard to find anything around here that is easier seen. And the story about how grandmother Ballantine named the place is pretty thin, also pretty safe for grandpa since grandmother is no longer around to verify or deny. The name "Casa Evidente" seems more appropriate, I think. Unless, of course — and this is what now intrigues me — the house is not the thing that is "well hidden."

If that is actually the case, then whatever is hidden here or near here must be very important, quite valuable, maybe even dangerous. How else can one account for grandfather's refusal to leave this godforsaken place and for Dr. Black's strange actions!

Maybe the valuable "well-hidden" thing is the loot from the stage holdup near the entrance to Castle Cap. He said the gold taken from the stage was never recovered. It would seem probable that the bandits might have buried it in the immediate vicinity because it was too heavy to take with them on horseback. And that grandfather, years later, somehow found the treasure. But none of this makes any sense, really, unless the amount was much more than the $10,000 grandpa mentioned. And how does Dr. Black possibly fit into such a picture!

If I have an opportunity, I think I will ask Dr. Black about the stagecoach thing. He will be out at the ranch while grandpa is in Fort Worth. Maybe I can ask Mr. Mac-Pherson, too, and see if all three stories match.

Another thought. The trip to Fort Worth, grandpa says is to discuss with his attorneys the revision of ranch leases to include reserving all mineral rights and the right of access to develop minerals. Could this mean that there might be a valuable body of ore of some kind or another underneath the ranch! But that is most unlikely. Why would he wait so long to do something with it!

The more I try to put the pieces of this puzzle together, the less they seem to fit. And how much of the answer, if any, does Ruth Hazelton know! I am sure of one thing. She wants me gone from this place.

Mr. Thatcher will be coming in a few days. I can hardly wait. Maybe, since he is a total stranger to the situation, I can somehow confide in him, possibly seek his advice. I can talk to you, dear diary, but it is a one-way conversation. And not enough.

She stared at the last page for a few moments, wondering if it might be a mistake to put her thoughts in writing. Certainly she felt better for having done so, but had it been wise? Suppose someone prowled through her belongings, found the diary and read tonight's entry? That possibility was too remote to be considered. She closed the hasp and returned the diary to the snap-down compartment.

As she was about to close the suitcase, she noticed a short thread protruding from the edge of the lining. It was almost an inch long and the same color as the lining. From her travel sewing kit she brought out scissors and snipped off the thread. She was about to discard it when she realized that it could be useful. Unfastening one of the two snaps, she slid the thread under the flap. It lay against the side of the metal snap and when the snap was fastened, about a quarter-inch of the thread was visible.

If anyone opened the compartment, she thought, they would not notice the thread and if they did notice would not attach any significance to it. She was sure that the unfastening of both snaps and removal of the diary would dislodge the thread or change its position noticeably.

Pleased with her ingenuity, she carefully slid the suitcase under the brass bed and returned to the writing desk. It would be advisable, she thought, to produce a couple of letters to account for her time. She wrote a brief note to her attorney, acknowledging his letter and authorizing him to pay several small bills. The second letter she wrote to a college friend.

Returning downstairs, Jamie saw that Ruth had finished reading the Fort Worth papers and was talking to Annie in the kitchen. The domino game was still going on in an air of intense concentration, broken only by the sound of shuffling dominoes at the end of each game.

Because there seemed nothing much else to do, Jamie began looking over the newspapers which were still carrying lengthy interviews with survivors of the *Titanic* disaster a month earlier. An editorial dealt gravely with the consequences of the split in the Republican Party. Another argued that the United States Marines should be sent to Nicaragua.

Finally, when it was nearing 10 o'clock, she asked to be excused and returned to her room. Tomorrow, she thought as she climbed into bed, would be a good time to do a little exploratory probing into Dr. Black's background. If she kept him talking long enough, it was possible that he might say something that would throw a little light on his place in the mystery of Bien Escondido. She would have to be very careful. The man was certainly no fool and if he showed signs of suspecting her intent she would have to back off quickly.

Why, she suddenly realized with a little thrill of pleasure, it was almost like planning a military campaign. Except that in a military campaign, one had an enemy and in this case she was not certain who it might be or, in fact, if there were an enemy. And a military campaign had a definite goal like the summit of San Juan hill. Where this one was headed, she had no idea.

CHAPTER 8

Sunday dawned bright and clear and gave promise of a fine, cool day. It was not a "church" Sunday and they would not be going into Goodland but would remain at the ranch and enjoy a leisurely Sunday dinner. Ruth had explained that she and Ballantine and Annie customarily went to town for church services, weather permitting, at least one Sunday each month. On such occasions, Dr. Black, as usual, would come out to keep an eye on the ranch while they were gone. He did not mind, Ruth said, because he only attended church services twice a year at Christmas and Easter.

It occurred to Jamie that any conversation with Dr. Black about his background ought to be as low-key as possible and just between the two of them. It would not be easy to do at the ranch house, she thought. But the answer came as a sudden inspiration — the promised ride in the new Packard. Surely, if Ruth had been correct, the doctor would not be able to resist the temptation to show it off.

"Dr. Black," Jamie said as Annie was clearing the breakfast table, "it's such a nice morning. I've been looking forward to a drive in your new car. You promised, remember?"

"Indeed I do. I was thinking of a solitaire session but that can wait until afternoon. Your idea is much better. Let's go right now if you're ready. Don't wear a hat. Just tie something around your hair. The top's down, you know.

"There's really no place where I can give you a decent demonstration, Jamie," Black said as they drove away from the ranch house. "I think we'll go south from the ranch gate. It's a fair road and anyway you have seen the country north from here to town two or three times."

The road south was reasonably straight and considerably smoother than the opposite direction and the car was soon travelling, Black said, about forty-five miles an hour.

"Notice how quickly we picked up speed," he said. "I can't go anywhere near full out but you can see what she's got. And how quiet the motor is. You don't notice the bumps, either."

Jamie turned to look at Black. The doctor was actually beaming with pride. Well why not, she thought. The man had no wife, no family. He had to have something to be fond of.

They were well south of Castle Gap now and the doctor pointed out several other landmarks: King mountain, Table Top mountain and a distant lake. Suddenly he pulled the car to the side of the road and stopped.

"I was afraid of that," he said after an inspection of the tires. "Thought I could feel it pulling. The right front tire is going flat."

From a tool box on the running board Black took several wrenches and a jack and dismounted the spare tire. In a way, Jamie thought, it was a fortunate occurrence since her planned conversation would be much easier without the wind rushing by her ears.

"You know, Dr. Black," she began tentatively, "I think it's really remarkable. Your relationship with grandpa, I mean. It's something a person seldom sees. Somehow it seems more than close friendship, almost like blood brothers or maybe a compact or covenant of some kind."

Dr. Black did not reply but paused a moment in placing the jack under the axle. Then he slowly pumped the handle. Jamie could feel the car rise. She could not see his eyes, but sensed that she had touched a nerve. Probably, she thought, she had gone too far too fast. It had been her intention to move gradually but somehow she had blurted out words she had not meant to use. It was a poor start, she thought, but nevertheless there had been some shock value to it. Dr. Black had reacted, if only by pausing a few seconds and by delaying any reply.

"Nothing really remarkable about it, Miss Jamie," Black said as he began to remove the punctured tire. "Everybody needs a best friend. I'm his and he's mine. It's that simple. In my case, I have no family at all out here and I guess your grandfather, and your grandmother while she was living, filled that void."

"Did you know grandpa before you came out here?"

"Yes, but not well. I was living in Denton, in northern Texas. My father who was also a doctor, had established a medical practice there after the war. Your grandparents were living in Austin at that time and I was introduced to them when I was in that city briefly. We seemed to think alike, most of the time, and exchanged correspondence fairly regularly.

"Then around 1890 I got a letter from your grandfather. He had come out here from Austin, bought some land and was going to start ranching. He was full of enthusiasm for the place and urged that I come out and hang my shingle in Goodland. And I did it."

It made sense, Jamie thought, and was not at variance with anything her grandfather had said. Probably it would be best to drop the questioning. At least for now. She had discovered one thing, though. Her first question had noticeably disturbed the doctor. She was more certain than ever now that her grandfather, Dr. Black and Bien Escondido were tied together by some bond that defied explanation. But there was more to it than personal friendship, politics, the price of cattle or the perpetual domino game.

The spare tire was mounted now and Dr. Black let the jack down and put away the tools. "Let's hope," he said, "that we can get back to the ranch without another flat. I don't relish having to patch a tube at the side of the road."

The drive back to the ranch was almost barren of conversation despite one or two efforts by Jamie. Dr. Black had become quiet, a development which she found disconcerting.

Following dinner and the after-dinner cigars, Black announced that he wanted to patch the punctured tube and pump up the tire before starting back to town.

"Would appreciate it if you could give me a hand, John," he said. "Sometimes it's a little difficult to get the tire back on the rim, particularly if it is a nearly new tire and this one is."

Ballantine agreed and the two men drove the Packard to a small building next to the bunkhouse which had been the ranch shop and still contained a workbench and assorted tools. The tire was dismounted from the rim, the tube removed and enough air pumped in to find the leak.

"I think I should mention a couple of remarks your Jamie made this morning, John," Black said as he removed a scraper, patch and rubber cement from the tool box. "It may be my imagination but I think she is digging for information."

"What did she say?"

"It was mostly her choice of words, John. She was commenting on the close relationship between us. The words she used were 'blood brothers' and 'compact.' She also used the word 'covenant,' and I find all of these most disturbing. She hit the nail on the head even though I think she was swinging in the dark."

Ballantine was silent for a few moments.

"I think," he said choosing his words carefully, "that you are getting yourself unnecessarily worked up about what is probably no more than youthful curiosity. When I was that age, and I am sure you were the same, if I came upon circumstances that puzzled me, I inquired about them. Later I got smart enough to talk less and listen more."

Dr. Black was not reassured. "I just wish that September would hurry up and that your Jamie were happily teaching scales to a bunch of kids back in Missouri. She's a fine girl but too curious. And that geologist or whatever he claims to be, just plain scares me to death. I tell you, John, the man is on to something. He'll have to be watched constantly right up to the time he high-tails it out of here."

The two men finished mounting the patched tube and tire on the rim, working in silence, and took turns pumping it up to full pressure. As they were ready to drive back to the house, Ballantine said, "Let's let it rest for a while, Morgan. You're beginning to make me feel uneasy and it's a feeling I don't like. I've been thinking about the situation for the last couple of days and I think I've figured out how we ought to proceed."

"Go ahead," Black said. "I've got an idea or two of my own but let's hear yours."

"I think, Morgan, that we ought to do nothing this summer, as you have suggested, and then go into action in September. Both Jamie and Mr. Thatcher will have left the ranch by then. As for Ruth, she has remarked from time to time recently that she would like to visit her relatives in Arkansas for a week or so. She has an aunt and uncle living in Little Rock and a flock of cousins. Counting travel time there and back, she would be gone from Bien Escondido for at least two weeks, maybe longer."

"And Annie?" Black asked.

"Annie would be happy to have two weeks off with pay. If I took care of the railroad tickets she might agree to spend the time visiting her other sister who lives in Fort Worth. That would be preferable to having her take the two weeks in Goodland. She could get back out to the ranch from Goodland on some excuse or other and arrive at an embarrassing time."

"I think it's a good plan," Black said after thinking for a moment. "Mostly because the Arkansas visit was Ruth's idea originally. It wouldn't look as if you were consciously trying to get her out of the way for a while."

"Ten days would give us plenty of time," Ballantine observed, "since we could work without interruption. And two weeks would provide a margin against any unforeseen delays."

"It's going to take some arranging in San Antonio, John. I think I should go there shortly after you get back from Fort Worth." Ballantine nodded agreement.

The two men returned to the house and immediately began the Sunday afternoon domino game. As the game began, Jamie excused herself and went to her room taking a book from the library and telling Ruth that she would read for a while and then nap for an hour or so.

The book was slow-moving and she couldn't concentrate. Instead, her mind turned to the perplexities she had uncovered and darted from one to another without finding satisfaction. She put the book down and stretched out on the bed, staring at the ceiling. A quatrain from the *Rubaiyat* suddenly came to mind: *There was a Door to which I found no Key; a Veil past which I could not see.*

"But the key is here. Right here in Bien Escondido," she heard herself say aloud and then wondered if anyone might have heard her. She went to the door quickly and looked out. Nobody in sight.

On a sudden inspiration, she pulled her suitcase from under the bed and carefully opened it. The thread was undisturbed. She removed the diary and carried it to the writing desk. After reviewing what she had put down the night before, she began to write:

> *May 23, 1912*
>
> *I was able to talk to Dr. Black today, away from the others here. We went for a drive in his new Packard. I was not as careful as I should have been in my choice of words and probably have both gained and lost as a result. Gained in that I am now certain that grandfather and Dr. Black are conspirators about something. Lost in that the doctor is definitely alerted and on guard against me.*
>
> *I believe it is best to keep a low profile for a while. Grandfather goes to Fort Worth the day after tomorrow and of course Dr. Black will stay here while he is gone. Maybe I can find some clue from his actions; perhaps some sort of pattern will develop. This whole thing gets more exciting every day. I just hope it doesn't turn out to be dangerous. For me, I mean.*

She closed the diary and returned it to the suitcase, carefully adjusting the loose thread, and slid it under her bed. As an afterthought, she positioned it so that one corner was exactly nine inches, as measured by a tape from her sewing kit, from the inside of the brass leg of the bed.

As she drifted gently into sleep, her last conscious thought was that on next Thursday afternoon, she could quit wondering what Dick Thatcher would look like. She would know. And she sensed in advance a warm and exciting moment.

CHAPTER 9

"I just can't get used to the idea of a farm — ranch, I mean — without a single milk cow or even a few laying hens," Jamie said reflectively.

"I'll admit it's a bit unusual," her grandfather replied. "But it makes sense when you stop to think about it. Back when the place was an operating ranch, before we leased the land, we did keep several cows for milking and your grandmother had a hundred or so chickens. There were five or six ranch hands most of the time and they liked their bacon and eggs. Fried chicken, too.

"After your grandmother was laid to rest in 1904, I lost interest in things for a while and disposed of all the livestock. Since then, as you know, I've leased out the land to other ranchers. As for milk and eggs, it is simple and convenient to buy what little we need at the Jim Richardson place on the way back from town. Cheaper, too."

Annie began clearing the breakfast table as they finished their coffee and Ballantine lit his morning cigar.

"Morgan will be out about 9 o'clock," Ballantine said, "and we probably ought to be on our way by 9:15. The eastbound train is due at 11:10 and that ought to give us about a half-hour to spare."

"You've got my shopping list, John?" Ruth asked.

Ballantine nodded.

It had been decided that Jamie would accompany her grandfather and Dr. Black to Goodland and Ruth had given her a list of three or four items to be picked up at MacPherson's store. Things were working out well, Jamie thought. This would give her an opportunity to visit privately with Andrew MacPherson.

Black arrived a little before nine, announcing that he had purposely allowed himself enough extra time to enjoy a cup of coffee before starting back.

"Here's the den key, Morgan," Ballantine said as they finished their coffee. "Remember I'm due back on the 29th. And Mr. Thatcher is due the day after tomorrow, the 27th. You and Jamie will have to meet the train and do the welcoming.

He glanced quickly around the room. Ruth and Annie were in the kitchen and Jamie upstairs but he lowered his voice. "I know it may be a little difficult for you, but try to make him feel welcome, at least until I get back. He's a guest here, after all."

"I will be the perfect surrogate host, John. You can depend on it. The last thing I want is for him to believe that I have any dark suspicion about what he is doing at Bien Escondido. I'll be charming and disarming."

A moment later Jamie came downstairs, a scarf tied about her hair, and she and Dr. Black went out to the car. The doctor had put up the top, she noted, probably because some heavy clouds were building up in the west. Ballantine joined them immediately, waving a goodbye to Ruth and Annie on the porch as the car moved smoothly out of the yard and onto the road.

The Fort Worth train was only five minutes late, a performance which was, according to Black, not quite a record but nevertheless remarkable. "It'll probably make up for it by being an hour late on the way back," Ballantine observed, earning a scowl from the conductor.

It was not quite 11:30 when Black stopped in front of MacPherson's store to let Jamie out. "I've a few errands to run, Miss Jamie. They'll take until 12 or so. If it's agreeable, we can meet at the Texan at 12:30."

"Take whatever time you need, Dr. Black. I'll wait in the hotel lobby if I'm there first."

MacPherson greeted her warmly and, after filling the shopping order, escorted her to his office.

"Talking with you, Miss Jamie, is almost like going home again. I haven't been back to Missouri for a long time now and Lord knows I'm not much of a hand to write letters."

"You really ought to take a vacation from this place, Mr. Mac-Pherson, and go back home for a week or so."

"Don't think so, Miss Jamie. You see, this is my home and has been for years. I'd be a stranger back in Missouri now. Wouldn't feel comfortable."

"Well," Jamie said, "I guess I'm pretty much a stranger here but I don't feel at all uncomfortable."

"Speaking of comfort, how do you like ranch life? And what do you think of Pecos country?"

"Bien Escondido isn't exactly my idea of a typical cattle ranch, Mr. MacPherson. Frankly, I find it somewhat boring. There's really nothing much to do. It's different for grandpa, of course. His roots and his memories are all there, and deep.

"As far as the Pecos country is concerned, it's fascinating. Why, only last week grandfather showed me a place on the old trail just a short way west of Castle Gap where bandits had held up a stage and gotten away with the strongbox and $10,000 in gold. It was never recovered, he said. Do you know anything about that?"

"Only that I didn't do it, Miss Jamie," MacPherson joked. "Yes, I've heard the story. There are several versions and about the only thing certain is that there really was a stage holdup near the Gap. The amount of the loot was probably exaggerated. It usually was in those days. Whether it was carried away or buried nearby is anybody's guess. There are those who think the gold was stashed away near the scene of the holdup and that the robbers never made it back to recover it. Your grandfather, I suspect, is one of the believers in the hidden treasure legend."

"He also showed me a place much closer to the ranch house," Jamie continued, "near the head of the little lake where he said Indians had attacked and burned several wagons sometime in the 1860s. You could still see a few of the wagon irons when he got here he said, but they're gone now."

"Don't recollect I ever heard that one," MacPherson replied. "It could be, though. Lots of things like that happened in the early days with hardly a scrap of evidence left behind. You figure to spend some time looking for the stage loot?"

Jamie laughed. "I wouldn't have the slightest idea how to go about it," she said. "And anyway, maybe grandpa already found it. I'm joking of course," she added at the same time watching MacPherson's face closely.

"There are a few folks around here who might go along with that idea," MacPherson said. "Especially since they see that your granddaddy lives very well without having to operate the ranch. Don't misunderstand me, Jamie, I'm not one of that group. I have never felt any urge to speculate as to other folks' business, what their income might be or where it came from."

It was time, Jamie thought, to change the subject.

"If I go looking for anything this summer, Mr. MacPherson, it might be... well, I don't know exactly what. Some sort of evidence of people who occupied this area long before the Indians came."

"Oh, yes, the young college professor. I had forgotten. I met him last summer when he was here briefly. I understand he plans to spend a few weeks at the ranch. Are you going to sign on as his helper?"

"Frankly, I haven't been asked. But it would be fun. At least it would break the monotony. He's due here on the 27th."

Jamie glanced at the octagonal clock on the wall behind the office

45

desk. 11:55. Explaining that she was to meet Dr. Black at the Texan, she thanked MacPherson for his help and was escorted to the door.

"Keep me posted on developments in the prehistoric research area," MacPherson said as Jamie departed. And also any romantic develpments, he thought. Young Thatcher was a handsome devil if he recalled correctly.

Returning to his office, MacPherson worked the combination on the steel safe in the corner and removed a small black notebook. Turning to the page carrying the current date, he made a single entry: "Wagon irons, head of lake. Jamie B."

Dr. Black's errands had taken less time than expected. He was sitting in the Texan lobby when Jamie arrived. While they were waiting to be served in the dining room, the doctor asked Jamie if she had thought of anything interesting that she might do during the summer.

"Why yes, Doctor," she replied, moved by a totally unexplainable inspiration. "I'm going to look for gold. Hidden treasure."

Black stared at her, unblinking, for a long moment. Then he gently cleared his throat and glanced through the nearby window and out into the street before replying.

"You have some definite...ah, target...in mind, Miss Jamie?"

It was, Jamie explained, the legend of the Butterfield stage holdup. She described in detail what her grandfather had told her and added that MacPherson had verified the story.

"I'm familiar with the matter," Black said, "but only that it is one of many legends of the area. Assuming there is something, somewhere, to be found, just how do you propose going about looking for it? You can't just grab a pick and shovel and dig under every bush and rock for miles in all directions. You would need a thousand helpers and ten years' time."

"Plus bushels and barrels of just plain luck," Jamie said, "but I've a much different plan in mind. I'll use a metal divining rod. They're much like the ones used to find underground water supplies except that they don't locate water — they locate metal."

"You have such an instrument?" Black inquired.

"Not here, Doctor. I'll have to write back home and have one sent. A family friend — he must be eighty years old by now — makes them. He uses a special kind of wood aged just right and shaped in a certain manner. Then he rubs in a concoction brewed from several herbs. He won't tell what they are. Says he learned the whole process from a gypsy family when he was a boy. He calls it a Treasure Witch."

"How does the thing work?" Black asked.

"There's a little slot in the wood, just above where it forks and you slip a piece of the metal you are hunting into that slot. If you're looking for silver, you would put a silver dollar; for gold, a half-eagle. Then you just follow the direction and intensity of the pull."

"Have you ever seen the thing work — or worked it yourself?" Black wanted to know.

"Yes, once. I found a horseshoe buried six inches deep in a pasture. I was showed a large oak and was told a horseshoe had been hidden within fifty feet of the tree. That would make a circle a hundred feet across. I found it in less than two minutes. When I got fairly close the pull was so strong that the rod almost seemed alive. It twists and turns so much you can scarcely hold on to it."

"This is most interesting, Miss Jamie," Black said. "I'll be looking forward to seeing this...device...when you get it. I have heard that there were people who claimed to have metal-divining ability but I never really took much stock in the idea. Those who said they had the power always seemed to be as skinny as church mice and practically camped at the door of the county poorhouse."

"All I know is what I've seen with my own eyes, Dr. Black," Jamie said, suddenly annoyed at the turn of the conversation. "You can think what you wish, but I know what I saw and felt."

They finished the meal in silence and had little to say on the way back to the ranch. The cloud bank that had been visible in the west was now moving in with intensity, announcing its arrival with a gust of wind laden with a stinging mixture of sand, dust and debris. The first large drops of rain fell as the car halted in front of the porch and Jamie dashed inside struggling to keep her feet.

Later, in the quiet of her room, Jamie reviewed the day's events. It was difficult to believe what she had done or to understand why she had done it. The entire story of her intention to spend the summer looking for the stage loot had been hatched right there at the dinner table, including the ridiculous account of the Treasure Witch and her testing of it in a Missouri pasture. All pure fantasy — or more precisely, a big, bald lie. Even so, she was pleased and a little surprised at the scope of her imagination and her mental agility. She had tossed a total fabrication at the man. And apparently gotten away with it.

Dr. Black's reaction had been revealing. He had been noticeably shaken. It was not, she felt, a normal reaction. One might expect a person to be amused or politely tolerant or even honestly interested. But the doctor had been deeply disturbed. The puzzle pieces were moving closer together.

Her diary entry that evening was brief:

Grandpa left for Fort Worth today. Dr. Black and I took him to the train. I suppose I ought to be ashamed of myself for the story I told the doctor while we were having dinner at the Texan but I am not. He thinks I'm going to hunt buried treasure on the ranch this summer and for some reason doesn't like the idea at all. There must be a connection between this and his being here whenever grandpa is gone. Are the two of them watching over something! If so, what is it! And where is it!

She carefully returned the diary to its compartment and arranged the thread. It's almost like setting a mousetrap she thought. And once more she measured the distance from the corner of the suitcase to the inside of the brass bed leg — nine inches.

As she fell asleep that night, she realized that the rain which had begun in midafternoon was still coming down heavily. Tomorrow would be cool.

CHAPTER 10

"I think," Jamie said as they finished their breakfast coffee, "that I might go out to look for arrowheads today. The air is so fresh and cool that it's a pleasure to be out. Grandpa said he sometimes finds them just west of the Gap not far from where the trail ran."

"That's true," Black replied. "It is believed that Indian hunting parties favored that area long before it was a white man's stage road because the game trails were there. Naturally, a lot of arrowheads and probably some spear points got lost. You've chosen an ideal day to look."

"Why is that?" Jamie asked.

"Because of last night's heavy rain. It might expose something like an arrowhead. A strong wind has a similar effect, but a heavy washing rain is better. Would you like to have me take you part of the way in the car?'

"No, thank you. I'll walk. The exercise will be good for me and I've plenty of time. Maybe I'll take a couple of sandwiches along and plan to be back by 3 or 4 o'clock this afternoon."

"Well, there isn't much of any way you could get lost, Miss Jamie," Black said. "The road is so poor it nearly vanishes in places but you can still follow it without much trouble. Even if you should lose the road you can always look west — downhill — and see the circle of green that marks the lake and just head for it."

"How are you fixed for hiking?" Ruth asked. "Your feet, I mean. You will need something more than street shoes. You wouldn't get half a mile over these rocks."

"I think I'm all right," Jamie said. "My parents belonged to a little group that enjoyed taking Sunday afternoon hikes through the woods and fields. My mother had a pair of boots for those occasions and they fit me perfectly. I brought them with me."

"I have a small knapsack you could take, Jamie," Ruth said. "You could use it to carry your sandwiches and anything else you might want to eat. You should slip in a canteen of water, too. It isn't wise to go very far or very long without water in this country."

Refilling his coffee cup, Dr. Black left the table and went to Ballantine's den, announcing he had brought some new books from town and intended to read for two or three hours. Ruth and Jamie went to the kitchen and began preparing sandwiches.

"Has John given you any specific directions to the area where he has found arrowheads?" Ruth inquired.

"No," Jamie said. "Only that it was this side of the Gap."

"Do you think you can find the rocky outcrop at the edge of the trail where the stage bandits hid? John showed it to you, didn't he?"

"Yes, he did. And I'm sure I could find it because the old road makes a sharp bend there."

"That's right," Ruth said. "If you go about another hundred yards past the outcrop and then leave the trail and go about the same distance to the left, you will see a rocky area. That's the place to look."

After packing the knapsack, Jamie went to her room, changed to a suitable skirt and light sweater and slipped on her mother's hiking boots. Although they were heavy and somewhat clumsy, coming eight or ten inches above her ankles, she realized that they would offer valuable protection against the cactus.

'We'll look for you back by the middle of the afternoon," Ruth said from the door as Jamie left the porch. "Don't lose track of time and stay so long that we become concerned about you."

"Don't worry, Ruth. I'll probably get tired and come back sooner." If I don't come back for a month, I'm sure it would be too soon to suit her, Jamie thought.

The road paralleled the small arroyo which fed the lake. In places it followed the old stage road her grandfather had said, and in others departed from it.

At the head of the lake Jamie saw that the normally dry arroyo had been about two feet deep in water and that the level of the lake was considerably higher than it had been the day before.

The ground sloped gently upward for the first mile or so, but then began to rise, slowing her pace. The road crossed the arroyo a couple of times and the second one was now impassable by car. Here Jamie stopped to rest. She had come about half way.

Looking back, she found she could still see the ranch buildings. Escondido, indeed! she thought. The rim of green marking the lake was clearly visible as Dr. Black had said. She took a sip of water from the canteen and set out again.

Another half-hour of steady walking brought her to the sharp bend in the road and the rocks behind which the stage bandits had hidden. She should leave the road about a hundred yards beyond the sharp turn, Ruth had said. Jamie counted off a hundred paces and then threw in twenty more for good measure which she judged would be somewhere around a hundred yards. It was as good a guess as any.

She turned off the road to the left, following Ruth's instructions, and in a few moments came to an area where the vegetation was much thinner and large, flat rocks were scattered about. There was little doubt, she thought, that this was the place Ruth had described.

She decided to rest briefly before beginning her search. Seating herself on a flat rock, she opened the knapsack and took out the canteen and one of the sandwiches. As she ate, Jamie reflected on the outrageous story she had told Dr. Black the day before. She was only a couple of hundred yards from the holdup scene, she realized.

A new thought surfaced. She had brazenly told Black that she would write to Missouri and have a "Treasure Witch" sent out. Since the thing existed only in her imagination, how would she explain its non-appearance? Some plausible story would have to be invented. She could report in due time that the old gentleman was gravely ill or even had died. It would compound the lie, of course, but there was no help in any other direction, she thought, as she adjusted the knapsack and got to her feet.

Rather than wander about aimlessly, Jamie decided to follow a pattern. She selected a reference point, a rock larger than the others about fifty yards away. She would follow a line toward it carefully examining the ground in a strip four or five feet wide. When she reached the reference rock she would move over a few feet and reverse her direction, searching a strip parallel to the first one. The process could be repeated as long as she wished.

She watched the ground closely, looking up only now and then to check her course. There were numerous small stones on the surface and it would be easy to miss an arrowhead among them, she realized.

Ten minutes later she reached the large rock without having any luck. Somewhat discouraged, she felt her little expedition was going to end in futility. Probably, she thought, there were only three lost arrowheads in the entire area and her grandfather had found all of them.

Rather than reversing her direction she decided to move off to her right toward a spot a short distance away with no vegetation at all. She had just entered this area head down, to examine the ground when she heard the unmistakable sound. Jamie had never heard the warning buzz before but somehow, instinctively, she recognized it. *Don't move*, she told herself.

She saw it immediately, directly in front and not five feet away. The snake was in a tight coil, its evil head raised, its malevolent eyes fixed upon her. In the center of the coil, she saw the rapidly vibrating tail.

She began backing away, her eyes on the snake. When the distance between them was ten or twelve feet, she turned and ran wildly back toward the trail. Too late to stop, she saw in an instant of pure terror the second snake. This one was not coiled, but lay in an "S" curve next to one of the flat rocks. Her right foot came down a few inches from the snake. Its head flashed forward and Jamie felt the sharp blow just above her ankle.

Nearly overcome by surging waves of fear and nausea, she continued running, her only thought to get as far away as possible. She reached the old stage road, turned downhill and did not stop until she came to the sharp bend. Her heart was pounding furiously and she knew she could not go on.

Her mind was racing. From somewhere she recalled having read that any exertion was the worst thing a person could do if bitten by a snake. The heart, working at top speed, simply rushed the poison through the system faster. She must remain calm, make an incision where the fangs had pierced the skin and try to squeeze the poison out.

She sat up, unlaced her boot and removed her heavy stocking. No marks. She rubbed the skin from her toes to above the ankle, but nothing. She was certain it was the right foot. To be sure, she checked her left foot. Nothing.

Only one answer. She had seen the snake strike, had felt the impact. The heavy leather boot had saved her. For the first time she saw the spot of dampness not more than a couple of inches from the top of the boot. Venom from the snake's fangs.

She opened the canteen and carefully poured water on the spot to dilute and flush away the venom. Then she laced up the boots and started walking unsteadily down the road. She was emotionally drained and physically exhausted and walked at a slow pace. No need to hurry, judging from the position of the sun.

As the shock wore off, several thoughts came to mind — disturbing thoughts. She had walked into an area infested by rattlesnakes. How had she gotten there? Had she accidentally stumbled upon it? Not at all. She had been sent there with specific directions. By Ruth.

She pondered the situation. Should she blurt out everything including her suspicion? Her hurt and anger urged her to do so.

As she approached the house, she made the decision: she would say nothing. At least until her grandfather returned. If Ruth's actions had been deliberate and sinister, which Jamie was prepared to believe, the woman would not be told what had happened. At least not today.

Making a definite effort to appear composed, Jamie crossed the porch and entered the house. No one was in the living room but from her grandfather's den she heard the distinctive sound of cards being shuffled. Evidently Dr. Black had tired of reading and had turned to solitaire. Jamie sank down into one of the leather-covered easy chairs.

Ruth came in from the dining room. She had not heard Jamie's footsteps on the porch and appeared startled.

"You're home early, I see. Did you have any luck?"

A great deal more than you will ever know, Jamie thought to herself, but aloud told Ruth that she had found nothing. "I think grandpa must have found them all," she said, managing a weak smile.

"Why don't you go upstairs and rest for a while, dear," Ruth said. "You've walked six miles or so and must be very tired. I know I would be. And you look a little pale."

Ruth was watching her closely, Jamie realized. A good idea, she thought, to go immediately before her fragile composure fell apart. Rising, she thanked Ruth for her thoughtfulness, excused herself and went to her room. Removing only the heavy boots, she stretched out on the bed.

There were, she thought, three possibilities. The most charitable one was that Ruth was innocent; that she had no knowledge of rattlesnakes in that area. The second was that Ruth had inadvertently given incorrect directions or that Jamie had misunderstood them. Finally, Ruth could have deliberately, intentionally, sent her to a rendezvous with death. At the moment, the third possibility seemed most likely.

If Ruth were indeed capable of such a thing, she would surely feel no hesitancy about less violent conduct. That would include, Jamie thought, going through her personal things to see if she could find anything damaging to Jamie and help to send her away from Bien Escondido and back to Missouri — where she would be conveniently out of the way. There had been ample opportunity today.

She thought of her diary. Slipping off the bed, she inspected the suitcase. It did not look quite right. Its position seemed changed. Getting the tape from her sewing kit, she measured the distance to the inside of the brass bed leg. Seven and one-quarter inches.

With mounting fear, she pulled the suitcase from beneath the bed and opened it. Touching the snap-down compartment she felt the diary inside and noted, with relief, that the position of the tiny thread under the snap was undisturbed. The compartment had not been opened.

But the suitcase had definitely been moved. Possibly it had even been opened and then closed immediately when it appeared to be empty. Or Annie could have been dusting and cleaning her room.

She could check on that later she thought as she lay down again and quickly fell asleep.

CHAPTER 11

Jamie awakened early the next morning from sunlight streaming in her east window. She had apparently forgotten to pull the shade. It was too early to get up so she lay luxuriating in the soft embrace of the brown and yellow quilt her grandmother had made.

She had slept most of the previous afternoon coming downstairs only for the evening meal and then excusing herself and returning to her room early, explaining that she was still tired and had a slight headache.

Ruth made no further mention of the arrowhead expedition and Annie, as usual, did not enter into the conversation. Dr. Black, after asking politely about Jamie's search and expressing regret that she had found nothing, launched into a lengthy description of the book he had been reading. He was still on the subject when Jamie went to her room.

She slept soundly and it had been good for her. Yesterday's terrifying experience began to take on the unreal aspect of her buffalo stampede nightmare. Perhaps she should pretend it really had been only a dream. Certainly it would be easier to cope with than the reality of her feeling toward Ruth.

Jamie dozed off again but was soon awakened by sounds of Annie preparing breakfast and the aroma of freshly-brewed coffee. As she dressed, she organized her thoughts. She and Ruth and Dr. Black would be going in to Goodland in the early afternoon to meet the 2:15 train, leaving Annie to look after things at the ranch. She would put the memory of yesterday completely out of her mind, replacing it with the more pleasant anticipation of Mr. Thatcher's arrival.

Breakfast passed without incident, the conversation dominated by observations about the weather and a brief discussion between Ruth and the doctor about the impending arrival of their guest.

"I really don't know his plans," Ruth said, "and I think that John has no idea either. He may intend to scout around on foot or perhaps he will need some sort of transportation. There aren't many places you can get to with a car, at least on what few roads we have, and I'm sure John wouldn't be at all happy about striking out across country in the Oldsmobile."

"Well, surely he knows what the situation is," Black said. "After all, he was here last summer for a few days. If he needs something more than his two feet, he can arrange for a buckboard at the livery in town or maybe work something out with Jim Richardson. Point is, it's his problem, not ours."

After clearing the table, Annie conferred briefly with Mrs. Hazelton and then set out for the garden with two large pans. There were lots of beans that needed to be picked, she said, along with some tomatoes. Jamie volunteered her help, primarily to avoid contact with Ruth.

As they moved down the rows of beans, Jamie saw she had been presented with an opportunity to resolve at least one question which had troubled her since the previous evening. Casually, she shifted their conversation around to Annie's general household duties.

In response to Jamie's interest, Annie outlined her weekly work schedule. Among other things, she said that general cleaning on the first floor was always done on Wednesdays and on the second floor on Fridays. It was a schedule that Mrs. Hazelton insisted on, Annie said.

"I suppose it's a good idea," Jamie said, "to get things done in an orderly manner. You won't be sweeping or dusting upstairs this week until Friday. Is that right?"

"That's right, Miss Jamie. Except for looking after my own room, I haven't done a thing upstairs and won't until Friday."

That eliminated Annie, Jamie thought. And certainly Dr. Black would not prowl around upstairs when both Ruth and Annie were within sight and hearing. But someone had moved her suitcase. It had to have been Ruth.

After returning to the house with the morning's harvest, Jamie went to her room and penned a brief note to a hometown friend. In it she described the ranch and the countryside in general but made no mention of specific events. She would be sure that Dr. Black saw her mail the letter and hoped that he would assume it was the "Treasure Witch" request. Later she could dream up a suitable explanation for not receiving one.

After an early noon meal, Dr. Black brought the Packard around to the front a few minutes after 12 noon.

"You ladies can hold down the rear seat," Black said, "but only if you don't attempt to drive." Promising to withhold any comments, Ruth and Jamie seated themselves and in a moment they were on their way.

In Goodland, Dr. Black parked the car across the street from Virginia Dolan's dressmaking shop, Ruth having indicated that she needed to visit with Mrs. Dolan for a few minutes.

"The postoffice is just around the corner, isn't it?" Jamie asked. "I'll just run over there and mail this letter while we're waiting."

Errands accomplished, they proceeded to the station and found, surprisingly, the westbound train posted as "On Time."

"At least we won't have to sit around for the usual half-hour or so," Black said as he dusted one of the waiting room benches with his handkerchief. As he spoke, the train's whistle sounded in the distance and in a few moments, it rounded a bend, bore down upon the station and came to a grinding halt, the engine panting and sighing in exhaustion. An acrid cloud of sulphurous smoke drifted across the scene.

Jamie, Ruth and Dr. Black moved onto the platform as passengers descended. The first one down was a young man not more than five and a half feet in height and weighing at least two hundred pounds. His face was florid and pudgy with small, closely-set eyes.

Jamie's heart sank. It must be Mr. Thatcher. The man's gaze swept the station platform obviously expecting someone. But no, Ruth ignored him and was still watching the emerging passengers.

Two women with young children were next, followed by a middle-aged man with sample cases, obviously a salesman.

"There he is!" Ruth exclaimed.

It was almost too good to be true, Jamie thought. Six feet tall, slender but well-muscled. When introduced, he removed his hat revealing an unruly shock of sandy hair that Jamie felt a wild impulse to touch. His eyes were the deepest of blue, a tiny dimple was in his chin. Jamie felt her pulse increase and she hoped that her face would not flush and send premature messages.

Thatcher's clothing was a pleasing compromise of casual and conservative: a light brown summer suit still neatly pressed despite the long train ride and a white shirt with a western string tie. He had two large leather suitcases which he carried himself, declining Dr. Black's offer to help.

"Do you suppose," Thatcher said as they entered the car, "that we could stop at a hardware store on the way out of town? I need a few simple tools — long-handled and short-handled shovels and a pick."

"It's not necessary for you to buy anything," Ruth said, "unless you prefer. We have quite a collection of tools including those you mentioned. You are welcome to use any of them. Except the garden hoe and yard rake."

"No need to worry, Mrs. Hazelton. I'm not much of a gardener," Thatcher replied. As he spoke he smiled broadly and Jamie saw two additional dimples appear momentarily at the corners of his cheeks. She must stop looking so closely, she realized.

A strong crosswind was blowing, making conversation in the car difficult and little was said on the return trip. Upon arrival, Dr. Black drove directly to the bunkhouse.

"Might as well unload your things first, Mr. Thatcher," Black said. "Supper won't be on the table for a couple of hours. Come on over to the house after you get unpacked and settled in. We can sit on the porch and talk politics."

"I'd like that. Something else I'd like, too. Would you mind — all of you — doing away with the Mr. Thatcher business and just calling me Dick? I have to live with formality three-fourths of the year and I'd like a vacation."

"That's agreeable with me," Black said. "And you can address me as Morgan or Doctor. Just don't go overboard and call me Doc."

"And please call me Ruth if you don't mind," Mrs. Hazelton said.

"I guess I'm old enough to be your mother and entitled to a certain amount of respect but I really prefer informality. This is West Texas. And here we revised the rules of polite society to suit ourselves."

"And you, Miss Ballantine, must I call you that?"

"If you do," Jamie said, "I promise I'll put a Missouri hex on your summer's research and all your digging will be for nothing."

"Jamie it is, then. I'll just put my quarters in order. No need for anyone to come in. I remember the foreman's room from last summer."

Thatcher entered the bunkhouse looking back over his shoulder. He was looking directly at her, Jamie realized. His smile was for her alone. She felt a surge of emotion that she would remember forever.

Thirty minutes later Thatcher joined Morgan Black on the porch. He had changed to a pair of tan trousers and a white linen shirt with the sleeves rolled to just below the elbows.

"You look comfortable, Dick," Black said. "I daresay more so than you will be after a few days of knocking around in the cactus and mesquite. A man can get a bad sunburn out there particularly when he's been indoors for months. I hope you brought a suitable hat. One with a wide brim. If you didn't, you better borrow one of John's."

"Thanks, Doctor," Thatcher replied. "I'll probably do just that. I'm pretty well fixed up in the clothing line except for a wide-brimmed hat. No way I could pack one."

"I've been curious as to how you plan to go about your search for a pre-Indian culture in this area. We didn't get to talk very long last summer and the matter has intrigued me ever since. Surely you don't expect to find any surface evidence."

"Probably the only thing one could look for on the surface is a petroglyph; a rock carving, usually of animals or hunting scenes. Caves are excellent places to look but I don't know if there are any in this vicinity. I'll probably spend a few days looking and then try to pinpoint a possible habitation site. If I find a spot that looks like it's worth the effort, I would do some augering or other digging there. One would be looking for charcoal, burned bones, pottery shards and the like."

"But why this particular location, Dick?"

"Castle Gap has always been a primary migration route for game animals in the memory of contemporary man. Chances are that things were about the same a thousand years, two thousand years ago. It's a simple matter of the hunter, lacking any kind of transportation, wanting to be as close as possible to his prey."

Thatcher continued, "You understand, of course, that there is a good chance that no pre-Indian culture ever existed in this area or perhaps in any other area. It's really a shot in the dark.''

''I can believe it. But it should make for an interesting summer. You ought to join forces with Miss Jamie. She plans to scout around in the bushes too, looking for some stage loot.''

Thatcher nodded. ''Might be a good idea. We could form a summer partnership. If we find the stage treasure, I would get half the money. If we uncover a prehistoric culture, she would get half the glory.''

''I'm afraid Miss Jamie would be getting the short end of that bargain,'' Black said. ''When it comes to choosing between a bushel of money and a bushel of glory, I'll take the cash every time.''

''She probably wouldn't be interested anyway. Seems to be a pretty independent type,'' Thatcher said.

They were silent for a few moments. When Thatcher spoke again, he changed the direction of the conversation.

''When did you come to west Texas, Doctor?''

''Twenty-two years ago, in a couple of months, summer of 1890.''

''Have you always lived in Texas?''

''Since a few years after the War. I'm a native of Kentucky, practiced medicine in Kansas for three or four years, then joined my father in Denton, Texas. He was a physician too and had established his practice there in the fall of 1865. John Ballantine talked me into coming out here shortly after he moved here from Austin.''

Thatcher, deep in thought, did not reply. Instead, he excused himself saying he would stretch his legs down to the lake and back before supper.

On the shore, he tossed a few stones at a leaf floating twenty feet away. His mind was in a turmoil. Dr. Morgan Black's name had meant nothing to him, no more than if it had been Smith or Jones until ten minutes ago. All that had changed instantly. A red warning light flashed in his brain.

Morgan Black's father had been a physician and was practicing in Denton, Texas, in late 1865 and for several years after, he assumed. Right place and right time, certainly. Right man? Probably.

Late that evening in his room, Thatcher wrote a brief note to a friend in Dallas. He'd mail it when they went in Saturday to pick up Mr. Ballantine.

> Dear George:
>
> I need to ask a small favor. Would you please make inquiry among your numerous friends, and determine if a Dr. Morgan Black lived and practiced in Denton until about 1890. Also, if his father was a practicing physician in Denton in or about 1867. If so, was the father's name

HARVEY BLACK!

If you can get a reply to me in the next few days, I'll greatly appreciate it and will repay the favor somehow when I get back to civilization.

Things were developing at a rapid pace, he thought as he prepared for bed. In less than eight hours at Bien Escondido he had accidentally stumbled on a potential threat in Dr. Black.

And that delightfully attractive girl! Tomorrow, he thought, he would get to know her better.

CHAPTER 12

"Tell me more about this petroglyph business, Dick," Black said. "I've never heard of any rock carvings around here."

"The chances are slim and I don't expect to spend more than two or three days working in that direction. One thing, though. The constant process of weathering from rain, blowing sand, freezing and thawing, over many centuries, would wear the carvings down so much that it would make them unrecognizable unless you knew what to look for and where. Most likely, you'd fail to recognize significant evidence. That's why it's worth a try."

Annie cleared the breakfast dishes and they were finishing a second cup of coffee. Thatcher was wearing working clothing, tan cotton shirt and trousers and short leather boots. A small note pad and pencil projected from his shirt pocket. Except for that slightly academic touch, Jamie thought, he looked nothing like a college professor. A mining engineer perhaps or the foreman of a construction crew. An active rather than a passive man.

"Where do you plan to start?" Ruth asked.

"I'll work my way up the road with occasional side excursions, maybe all the way to the top. It will be mostly a general reconnaissance and I'll make notes of areas that I want to return to later."

As Thatcher spoke, Jamie resisted a growing impulse to volunteer to accompany him. He had invited such a suggestion by referring casually during breakfast to her plans for what he called "the stage loot." But such obvious eagerness would be premature. Next week would be much better.

"Well, I'm off," Thatcher said as he left the table. "Look for me back in the late afternoon."

"Would you mind if I walked along for a short way?" Black asked. "Maybe a hundred yards or so. The exercise will do me good. I promise not to ask a lot of fool questions."

Thatcher hesitated before replying. "Of course, Doctor. Glad to have you. And I don't mind questions."

It was a polite but not completely sincere response, Jamie realized. Thatcher had not been pleased by Black's joining him, even for a short time. Perhaps he hoped Jamie might be the one to offer her company and for the moment she regretted not having done so. She could have walked as far as the lake, she thought.

More likely he didn't want anyone at all. Maybe the man was a loner. For whatever reasons, it was apparent that Black was not welcome.

As the men left the ranch yard and started down the road, she watched until they reached the head of the lake where the road turned slightly to the left and began following the arroyo. Then she went to her room.

Friday morning. Cleaning time for upstairs bedrooms on Annie's weekly household duty schedule, she thought. Sure enough, minutes later Annie came up the stairs, turned down the hall and stopped at her door.

"Mind if I start here, Miss Jamie?" she asked.

"Not at all. Could I help with dusting furniture?"

"No need, Miss Jamie. Just set and keep me company. Miss Ruth's gone out to pick a few garden things and turn some water to her flowers, so I'd be alone up here if it weren't for you."

Surprisingly, the first thing Annie did was to pull out Jamie suitcase. She ran her carpet sweeper back and forth several times under the bed and then returned the suitcase. It was now several inches away from its original position Jamie could see, confirming her belief that anyone moving the suitcase would not get it back exactly in place.

Annie moved to the south end of the room with her carpet sweeper, methodically working her way across the room. Obviously, Jamie thought, if there were to be any conversation, she would have to initiate it.

"Don't you get a little bored being tied to the house?" Jamie asked. "Do you ever feel the urge to go hiking in the brush, maybe up to Castle Gap or over to King mountain?"

Annie paused before replying, leaning lightly on her sweeper handle. "Not really, Miss Jamie. I figger I haven't lost anything out there and I don't have any hanker to go farther than down to the lake. Anyway, I reckon I'd be scared to go alone."

"What's to be afraid of, at least in daytime? Are there scorpions?"

"Yes, they's scorpions, but they ain't any trouble unless you're camping out. Then they sometimes get in your bedding or your shoes and can sting you good."

"How about rattlesnakes?"

"Two kinds, Miss Jamie. One kind is the little, short fat ones called sidewinders because of the funny way they move. Not many around here. They like sandy places. Farther west toward the Pecos there are supposed to be quite a few."

"And the other kind?"

"Diamondbacks, Miss Jamie. Big and mean. Only place I know of where they's diamondbacks for certain is up toward Castle Gap. Diamondbacks like rocky places. You can tell when you're in snake country 'cause of the rocks all around and not much grass or brush. Stay away from places like that. They're out mostly at night. They hunt then and hole up in the daytime. Best be careful any time."

Jamie thought back to when she and Ruth were preparing sandwiches for the arrowhead hunting expedition. Annie was well aware of the "snake country" near Castle Gap. Why hadn't she spoken up?

She concentrated. Who had been standing or sitting where, doing what, when the conversation occurred? She could place herself, seated at the end of the table nearest the outside door. Ruth had been standing by the cabinet on the south wall, opening a jar of jam. And Annie had been...where?

Suddenly she realized Annie hadn't been there at all. Annie had gone to the bunkhouse as soon as breakfast dishes were done to tidy up the foreman's room for Mr. Thatcher.

Dr. Black had gone in to make his bed in the den, as he insisted. Didn't want to make extra work for anybody, he said. He had locked the den behind him as was also his custom, and then set out on his morning walk.

No one, then, other than Jamie and Ruth had been in the house. It would be her word against Ruth's.

There could be no doubt. Ruth had deliberately sent her to that rendezvous with terror. Certainly in the hope that it might so frighten her that she would return to Missouri. To make matters worse, Ruth had prowled through Jamie's room, moved and probably opened her suitcase while she was gone.

A black and ugly tide of anger rose in Jamie's throat. Realizing that her face must reflect this, she glanced at Annie who was finishing her dusting and gathering her things together. Impossible to know if Annie had noticed anything. . .probably not. It couldn't really matter.

By mid-morning, Thatcher and Dr. Black had reached a point a mile up the road from the head of the lake. Progress had been slow with frequent deviations to inspect rock outcroppings. Thatcher made brief pencil references in his notebook, but otherwise indicated he was finding nothing of interest.

"Any point in looking farther from the road?" Black asked.

"Possibly. But I don't plan to spend more than a couple of days at the most on the petroglyphs. As I said, chances are slim. Near the game trails would be the place to look. Around the lake would be a good bet too, although there's no way of knowing if the lake was in its present position or even existed at all a thousand or more years ago."

"Well," Black said, "I think I'll ease on back to the house. I'm about a third through an interesting book I started a few days ago and I want several more chapters under my belt before nap time. Good luck with your search."

As Black moved off down the road, Thatcher turned and walked east toward Gastle Gap. A good idea, he thought, to go all the way to the top so he would be familiar with the terrain in case anyone questioned him. He moved at a steady pace and, although he passed numerous rock outcrops, he made no effort to examine them.

Upon arriving at the ranch, Black went directly to the den, unlocked it and removed a book from his small valise. *ARCHAE-OLOGY FOR EVERYMAN* it was titled. He had borrowed it from a friend in Goodland who had an extensive private library. In the first five chapters he had found nothing that might discredit Thatcher. Unfortunately, the book concentrated on such places as the Mesopotamian plain, the sites of Troy and Carthage and the Egypt of the Pharaohs. No references to petroglyphs.

In retrospect, he regretted having mentioned to Thatcher that he was reading an "interesting" book. Suppose he asked to borrow it this evening. He would provide a substitute — something from Ballantine's own library that he had already read and was familiar with.

He was just finishing chapter seven when Annie knocked on the door of the den to announce dinner was on the table. The meal was uneventful and conversation limited. Perhaps it was only his imagination, Black thought, but Jamie seemed to be cool and withdrawn. When she spoke, it was to him. She avoided contact with Ruth. Probably they had some kind of argument during the morning. It was not his problem and he would stay out of it.

One o'clock was nap time in Black's normal routine and he returned to the den to sleep until nearly three. Following the nap he went to the porch, by then in shade, and sat down in one of the chairs facing the lake.

A sudden movement near the arroyo caught his attention. Thatcher. The man was walking slowly up the west bank, eyes to the ground, raking at the sand and gravel with a short stick. Now and then he would kneel and scratch with his hands. Black could not be certain but it appeared Thatcher was looking for something specific.

A thin smile formed on Black's face and he spoke in a voice almost inaudible. "If you're looking for what I think you are, my fine but phony archaeologist, they aren't there any more."

Late that evening in the kitchen of his modest home on Fourth Street, Andrew MacPherson sat immersed in thought. Although it was nearly 11 o'clock, and an hour past his usual bedtime, he was far from sleep. He had made a pot of coffee on the small kerosene burner that supplemented the kitchen range and had placed a cup on the table.

Suddenly he made the decision. He put a second cup on the table, left the kitchen, moved down the hall to the downstairs bedroom and opened the door. His wife, who had gone to bed at 10 o'clock, sat up sleepily.

"Emma, would you please put on a robe and come to the kitchen? I have a pot of coffee hot. There's something we must discuss."

Rubbing sleep from her eyes, she sat down opposite him as he filled her cup. "You always make it too strong, Andrew," she said after a cautious taste. "Are you sure this can't wait until morning?"

"I think not. This thing has been on my mind most of the last two or three days. So much so that I'm beginning to neglect business at the store. I've got to talk about it. Now.

"You are aware," he began," that for a number of years there has been speculation about John Ballantine. People have wondered how it was that he seemed to prosper when everybody else was losing his shirt. In the hard times of the '90s he had no problems. In fact, he was buying land. Lots of it. Where did the money come from? Surely not from his ranch operation which was never worth a thin dime in the best of years."

"I've heard he may have inherited wealth back east," Mrs. MacPherson said.

"I suppose. But that doesn't explain a lot of other things. The secrecy for example. He does his principal banking business in San Antonio and keeps only a small personal checking account at the

Cattleman's Bank here. And a law firm in Fort Worth handles his legal work. I tell you, the man is hiding something. Something big.''

''Why do you bring this up now, Andrew?''

''Because of a chance remark his granddaughter Jamie made in the store a couple of days ago. She said that John told her about finding burned wagon irons near the head of the lake just east of the ranch house when he first came here. She said several wagons had been attacked by Indians in the 1860s and burned there.''

''Couldn't that have happened?''

''I suppose so, yes. But isn't it strange that nobody seems to have heard of this except John Ballantine? I never heard of it and I reckon I know most of the stories and legends of the area. Yesterday I took a little time off and asked Jack Blake and Charley Easterday about it. Between the two of them, they constitute a local historical society. Neither heard of such a thing.''

''What do you think?'' Emma asked.

''What I think is that the wagon irons existed and had great significance. I think John was about to tell his granddaughter their true significance when he suddenly changed his mind for some reason and covered up with the Indian attack story. Can't say why I think this. Call it a hunch.

''There's more,'' he continued. ''I've known about this for several years and kept my mouth shut. Figured it wasn't my business. It seems that periodically the local bank gets a cashier's check from a San Antonio bank for the credit to John Ballantine's account. Nothing unusual about that, of course, except for one thing. The arrival of those checks invariably coincided with a trip to San Antonio by — guess who — Morgan Black. Dr. Black would leave for San Antonio and about ten days later a check would arrive at the Cattleman's Bank for credit to Ballantine's account. It never failed, four or five times a year, for at least a dozen years.''

''How did you come by this information?''

''I guess it doesn't matter if you know, Emma, but I will rely on you not to repeat it. Will Wright — he died last year you may remember — was assistant cashier at the bank. He told me and I am sure he would not have except that a couple of extra beers loosened his tongue one night. He came around the next day and asked that I forget what he had said. I have done it, until now.''

Emma MacPherson remained silent for a few moments, then arose and filled both cups.

''Andrew, as long as this is apparently open season on John Ballantine, I might as well toss in what I've heard. It's a little strange, too.

Their girl, Annie Murphy, told her sister in town here and the sister told a friend and the friend told me."

"If you're going to tell me that John and Ruth Hazelton share a bedroom," MacPherson said, "it would be no surprise."

"Not that at all, although I believe people generally consider that to be true. No, what Annie wanted to talk about was not a bedroom. It was a den. John Ballantine's den on the first floor."

"What's so strange about a man having a den?"

"Would you believe Annie has never been in that den, to clean it or for any other purpose, since she went to work there five or six years ago? And according to Annie, Ruth is denied access too. Ballantine dusts and cleans the place up himself. There's more, too."

"Go on, but I can't see anything unusual so far. The man probably keeps his business records in there and very likely some personal remembrances from his marriage. He could be sensitive about that."

"That's probably true, but here's the strange part. Guess who *does* have access to that den. Guess who shares possession of the only key. Guess who has a cot in the den and sleeps there when he's at the ranch, which is frequently, and without fail when Ballantine is gone."

"You've given me three guesses," MacPherson said. "One is enough. Dr. Morgan Black."

"All right," Emma said. "So where does that leave us? Wouldn't you say there is ample evidence of some kind of working agreement between Ballantine and Black? An agreement that must be a deep secret? An agreement that must almost certainly result in money flowing into Ballantine's bank account from San Antonio whenever Dr. Black goes to that city? And if your hunch is right, all of this is connected to the burned wagon irons at the head of the lake which have long ago conveniently disappeared."

MacPherson nodded agreement. "I'm glad I got you out of bed, Emma. You've helped tie things together. Question right now is, what to do about it. I want to think on the matter for a few days but my feeling is that the first thing we need to do is to check out what Black does when he goes to San Antonio. I have a friend there who has some surveillance experience. He could tail him from the time he leaves the train."

"Suppose you find out just what it is they're doing and why it must be so secret. What might that lead to?"

"An enlarged partnership, my dear. Ballantine, Black and MacPherson."

"And what would your contribution be?"

"Silence, Emma. My silence."

CHAPTER 13

Summer would be hot and dry, Ballantine thought as he stared at the passing landscape. The vegetation was not lush and green as it should be in late May. Particularly since leaving Abilene. And the Colorado was lower than it should be at this time of the year, too.

Turning from the window, he reviewed what he had accomplished in Fort Worth. He had explained his desire to create a trust fund for Jamie to the attorneys. They had made several suggestions about terms and recommendations as to a trustee. The trust fund amount was not known at the moment, he had told them, but would probably be somewhere between two hundred and three hundred thousand dollars. He had explained that everything would be in order to complete establishing the trust by the first of January and that he would come to Fort Worth the middle of December to transfer the funds and execute the documents.

He had also discussed his wishes concerning his last will and testament which his attorneys had prepared and he had signed in the presence of two witnesses.

"There is something you should understand, Mr. Ballantine," the senior attorney had said. "It is more than seven months before the end of the year when you expect to place a very substantial sum in trust for your granddaughter. Should you die, God forbid, between now and December, all of your planning concerning the trust fund would be to no avail. The will would govern. Therefore, we suggest that you do not delay but proceed immediately toward creation of the trust."

He had told them only that it would require several months to convert certain property into cash and that it would not be possible to proceed any faster.

The will should be filed with the probate court in Goodland without delay, the attorneys had said, and advised him to take care it was not misplaced or accidentally destroyed since it was the only signed and witnessed copy. He had placed it carefully in his suitcase between two shirts.

Ballantine glanced at his watch. The train was due in Goodland in about fifteen minutes but the conductor had said they were running ten minutes late. Suddenly he felt a severe pounding in his temples, a searing surge of heat. He started to his feet. Heads and shoulders of passengers in front of him evaporated in a whirling, white mist. He collapsed to the seat and then fell heavily to the floor of the car. His last conscious thought was that he had waited too long.

Dr. Black was annoyed because they had not left the ranch when he had planned. In fact, they had been delayed more than thirty minutes. It wasn't his fault. The Packard simply would not start until he and Thatcher had disconnected and cleaned the gas line to the carburetor. Dirty gas, probably, or maybe water in the line, he thought.

He was pleased that Thatcher had agreed to come in to meet the train. Better for him not to be left alone, except for Annie, for several hours at the ranch where he could pursue his explorations unobserved.

As they approached the edge of town, Black was surprised to see the train still standing in the station. Apparently it had been late too. As he parked the car in the shade at the side of the station, he noted a small group of people talking together on the platform. He sensed something was wrong.

"Wait here a moment," he said to Ruth and Jamie in the back seat. "I'll go and look for John."

As Black started down the platform toward the train, the station agent left the group and came to meet him.

"Morgan," he said, "I'm sorry to tell you this. John Ballantine is dead. It happened less than an hour ago. All very sudden and without warning according to the conductor and passengers who were near him. He must have had a massive stroke or heart attack."

Black was unable to speak. Then with a determined effort, "Is he . . . is he still on the train, Arthur?"

"No, Doctor. They've taken him to Sanderson's Funeral Parlor. Dr. Adams was called. He examined John and pronounced him dead. Said that death had probably occurred almost instantly and painlessly. Adams accompanied the body to Sanderson's. They've been gone only five or ten minutes."

Black turned and walked slowly back to the car, his mind numb. A hundred thoughts struggled to emerge but he put them aside. There was, at the moment, only one great, overpowering truth. John Ballantine was dead.

"Something's wrong," Jamie said. "Where's grandfather?"

Black came to the side of the car and put his hand on Jamie's shoulder. "He's not going to be with us any more, Miss Jamie," he said, instantly aware that he should have said it better.

Jamie did not reply but sat staring at Morgan Black almost without comprehension. *This just cannot be,* she thought. *Not again, in only a few short weeks. It must be another nightmare.* But she was not dreaming, she knew. It was reality and she must not fall apart.

"What happened?" she asked. Black repeated what the station agent had said.

"Can we go to him?"

"Yes, I think so. Maybe I should check on his things before the train pulls out. Do you know what luggage he took with him?"

"Only one suitcase," Ruth said. "A large, brown leather bag. It had his name on it."

The suitcase was already inside the station ticket office. There had been no packages or other personal effects on the train according to the agent. Black placed the suitcase in the luggage rack and turned to Jamie and Ruth.

"We can go on over to Sanderson's now if you feel up to it," he said. "There will be a few decisions to be considered this afternoon."

Both Ruth and Jamie silently nodded agreement and without further conversation Black drove to the Sanderson establishment, a large brick building three blocks north of the Texan Hotel on a corner. A sign in bold letters stated: **Sanderson Hardware And Furniture.** On the side street wall, in equally large letters, **Undertaking — Caskets — Funeral Parlor.**

Donald Sanderson had seen Black's car stop across the street and was waiting at the door. After expressing condolences, he escorted them to a side door which led directly to the funeral parlor. Ballantine's body, in a wicker carrying basket, lay on a low table at the front of the room. A white sheet covered the body. Sanderson drew it back to reveal Ballantine's head and shoulders.

Jamie reached out and gently touched her grandfather's cheek, already translucently pale. "I'm so sorry, grandpa."

Ruth Hazelton began to weep softly and Morgan Black's eyes misted as Sanderson drew the sheet over Ballantine's heavy shock of grey hair.

"If you would all like to come into the next room," Sanderson said, "we can sit down and discuss how you wish to have things taken care of." He led the way into a side room where a small selection of caskets lined two of the walls with several chairs against a third.

"I'm not sure I should be here," Thatcher said, as the others were seating themselves. "I can wait in the car if you prefer."

"Please stay," Jamie said. "Even though you didn't know him

long, I am sure that you thought a lot of grandfather and he has spoken well of you."

"Miss Ballantine," Sanderson began, "I presume that decisions which are necessary will have to be yours. As I understand, you are John's only living relative. Can you tell me if he left any instructions as to details? Where he wished to be interred?"

"He told me once," Jamie replied, "that when his time came he wanted to be buried next to grandmother on the ranch."

Ruth Hazelton nodded agreement. "I've heard him say it many times, Mr. Sanderson," she said.

"It's what John would want, I'm sure," Black added.

"Then that is settled," Sanderson said. "I would suggest the day after tomorrow at two in the afternoon. I will send men out tomorrow to open the grave. You should have the exact location selected so that you can show them. As to services," Sanderson continued, "they could be arranged in his church or we have a small private non-denomination chapel right here in the building, if you would prefer."

No one spoke for a moment. Then Dr. Black said, "If I may make this suggestion, I believe John would have preferred as simple a service as possible. In fact, he said to me once, 'Don't let them haul me into any church, Morgan, and sing an off-key *Rock of Ages.'* I think a short, simple graveside service with some of his old friends present and a prayer by the Presbyterian minister is what he would have wanted."

"Then that's what we will do," Sanderson said. "I'll speak to Reverend Jackson about it.

"Now, concerning pallbearers, I'm sure John would want you, Morgan, to head the list. Would you care to suggest others?"

Black thought a moment and then named several of Ballantine's friends. Sanderson could contact them, he said.

The selection of the casket, Jamie's decision, brought tears to her eyes for the first time. She chose one of solid oak, simple in design. Her grandfather would have wanted something sturdy and substantial.

"I don't believe there is anything more that needs to be done this afternoon," Sanderson said. "Unless you, ah, would prefer that he be dressed in some other suit for burial."

"He was fond of the suit he was wearing today, Mr. Sanderson," Ruth said. "I think that's what he would like."

"One other thing," Sanderson said. "He has on what appear to be new boots. Expensive ones."

"Yes," Jamie said. "He planned to get them on this trip. I think they should stay with him."

Sanderson escorted them back to the funeral parlor asking that they excuse him for a few moments. He returned with a small parcel which he handed to Jamie.

"Personal effects from John's clothing, Miss Jamie. There was his bill fold containing $110, his watch, a gold ring, some pocket change and keys. There weren't any papers of any kind."

Jamie murmured her thanks.

Sanderson turned to Black. "Doctor, I'd appreciate it if you would plan to be here about 11:30 and take three or four of the other pallbearers in your car. Reverend Jackson can ride with me. As you know, I got a new motor hearse last month and retired the horse-drawn hearse. You will follow me at the head of the procession from town. I figure we ought to allow two hours."

The drive back to Bien Escondido was barren of conversation, everyone deeply immersed in private thought. Following supper and after Annie, eyes red from crying, had gone to her room, Dr. Black suggested they confer around the dining room table.

"There are a few things that will have to be considered and decisions made," he said, "as soon as John has been laid away. I don't want to appear to be rushing things and we shouldn't. But you can at least be thinking about them. One of the first things is the matter of John's estate I'm not a lawyer, but I would assume that you, Miss Jamie, are the sole heir. It will be up to you, I guess, to contact an attorney in this county and get a probate of the estate started. Until you do, his funds would not be available to pay various necessary expenses

"John told me recently that he had never made a will and I assume that he died intestate. An administrator will have to be appointed by the probate court before much of anything else can occur and I will be glad to serve in that capacity if you desire, Miss Jamie. I think John would have wanted me to. We can discuss this next week.

"The next thing is what is to be done about looking after the ranch. As you all know there is nothing requiring my presence in Goodland. I'll be glad to move out here and take care of things during the summer and into fall if necessary. I'd want to be back in town before winter.

"Now, please forgive me if it appears that I am trying to make plans for everybody. It's just that these thoughts have occurred to me and I think they should be tossed out for consideration.

"I believe, Miss Jamie, that you should go back to Missouri as soon as the estate proceedings are under way. You would be with your close friends and I am sure that you have many. This isolated ranch is no place for a young woman alone, or even if both you and Ruth were here, which I do not consider safe or advisable."

He turned to Ruth.

"Mrs. Hazelton, John told me just a week or ten days ago that you have been wanting to spend some time in Little Rock with your cousins and family friends. In fact, he said he planned to suggest that you go this summer. In view of the circumstances, it seems to me that you should spend a few days getting the house in order and then go there. You should perhaps plan to stay until fall. By that time the estate proceedings should be about complete and Miss Jamie will probably have decided what disposition she wants to make of the ranch.

"Annie should go in to Goodland and possibly seek other employment. As I said, I can stay out here during the summer and take care of anything that needs to be done."

No one spoke for a long moment. Then Jamie said, "I don't believe we should attempt to decide these things — any of them — until after the funeral services. Next week will be soon enough and maybe we can see things in the light of logic and not of emotion."

"You're right, of course," Black said. "It was perhaps premature for me to have made these suggestions at all, but it seemed sensible to consider what decisions lie ahead."

Thatcher spoke now, addressing Jamie rather than Morgan Black. "With respect to me and my proposed work, I'll do whatever is agreeable to you, Jamie. I'll stay on in the bunkhouse if you have no objection or I can pack up and go back east."

It was the first positive, strengthening thing that had happened to her since morning, Jamie realized. Although Black had been dominating the conversation, Thatcher had turned to her as the person in charge. Not to Morgan Black, not to Ruth Hazelton, but to her, Jamie Ballantine.

"Let's decide that next week, too," she said, offering Thatcher the hint of a smile as evidence of her gratitude.

Late that night, Jamie sat before her open diary. The last entry had been made on the 25th, the day Ballantine had taken the train to Fort Worth. It was almost unbelievable, she thought, how much had happened in four days. Dick Thatcher had entered her life. Her grandfather had departed from it. She began to write, slowly and thoughtfully.

> *Bien Escondido, May 29*
>
> *Grandfather Ballantine passed away very suddenly on the train returning from Fort Worth. He will be buried day-after-tomorrow, next to grandmother here on the ranch.*
>
> *I do not know if I can go on, having lost parents and grandparent in just a few short weeks. If I was an orphan yesterday, I am truly alone today, for grandfather was the only family I had left.*

But I MUST go on and right here on the ranch. It is the only home I have, anywhere. And not only that, I realized this evening that I AM Bien Escondido, just as grandfather was yesterday and for almost a quarter-century before that. Whatever it is that he was guarding here is my responsibility now and I intend to pursue that responsibility.

It will not be easy, I am sure, for I have enemies. Ruth Hazelton fears or hates me or both, sufficiently to deliberately place my life in grave danger. I must watch her carefully from now on.

And Dr. Black, that steadfast friend of grandfather. How quickly, how relentlessly, he tried to move into complete control this very day, only hours after grandfather's death! He is not as smooth a fox as I had imagined. He should not have permitted his eagerness to be so evident.

What he wants to do is to have me, as grandfather's only apparent heir, get a probate of the estate started immediately. Nothing wrong with that, of course. I know from my Missouri experience that it should be done without delay. He lost no time, however, in offering his services as administrator, hinting that grandfather would probably have wanted this. Most likely the court would appoint him, knowing how close they had been.

Then, as administrator of the estate, he would move into the ranch house for the summer and possibly into the fall in order to "take care of things" in his official capacity. And, to get everything neatly in place, he would have Ruth go to Little Rock for an indefinite visit, probably never to return. And it would be inappropriate, of course, for me to remain at the ranch. Hence his suggestion that I return to Missouri while the estate is being settled. Annie he would simply fire and undoubtedly he would ask Dick Thatcher to leave.

How nice for the good Dr. Black! How convenient! All alone at the ranch, clothed with the authority of administrator of the estate. Whatever secret project he and grandfather were engaged in, would now belong solely to Morgan Black and any move he wanted to make would be unobserved and without interference.

I'm going to have news for you, Doctor. This is my home and I'm going to stay here. What's more, to keep you properly frustrated, I'll ask Ruth to stay, if I have to *pay her myself. Annie too. I am not exactly destitute. I still have dad's life insurance money banked in Missouri.*

Most of all, I want Dick Thatcher to stay on during the summer. Is it wrong for me to feel so strongly after such a short time? I don't know; I only know that the feeling is there and that it is real.

She closed the diary, fastened the brass hasp and tucked it away in its hiding place, carefully arranging the thread under the snap as before.

Her last thought as sleep enfolded her was that a new chapter in her life was about to begin. A time of great challenge.

CHAPTER 14

Ruth Hazelton sat deep in thought. It was the next afternoon and she was in her bedroom. Earlier she had unpacked Ballantine's suitcase and put away his clothing and the small items she had asked him to buy for her.

She had found a large manila envelope. It was sealed with no printing or writing on it. Attached with a rubber band, however, was a note. In Ballantine's handwriting: "Attorneys' instructions are to file this with the probate court in Goodland and tell someone that it is there. This should be done immediately since it is the only executed and witnessed copy."

There was no question in Ruth's mind as to the contents. Although Dr. Black had said Ballantine had never made a will, that omission had obviously been taken care of in Fort Worth. She hesitated only a moment and then had taken the envelope to her room and locked it in her dresser drawer. She had thought of nothing else since.

Now she glanced at her bedroom door to assure it was bolted. She then removed the envelope from its hiding place and sliced it open with a penknife. The document which she removed bore in old English script the formal heading, *Last Will and Testament,* and began, In the Name of God, AMEN.

The will named Morgan Black as executor, subject to his acceptance and the approval of the court, and then proceeded directly to business. The sum of $5,000.00 in cash was bequeathed to her and $500.00 to Annie. All the remainder of the estate, both real and personal was to go to "my beloved granddaughter, and my only kin, Jamie Ballantine."

The last paragraph disturbed Ruth the most. "I wish to direct the attention of the court to the fact that my beloved wife, Margaret Ballantine, departed this life in the year 1904. I have not remarried, and any person claiming that any marital relationship exists, either by statutory law or by common law, is guilty of an untruth."

There could be no mistaking the target of those words, Ruth thought. They were meant to choke off any claim she might make about any intimate relationship.

Suddenly, she was pleased with her foresight a year ago in having discussed her situation with Victor Adamson. One of three attorneys living and practicing in Goodland, Adamson had a reputation for being honest and at the same time aggressive in behalf of his clients. Moreover, Ruth knew, he had demonstrated a definite coolness toward John Ballantine, for what reason she did not know, and she felt he would be completely on her side in the event of an adversary situation.

Adamson had told her that, in his opinion, there was ample support for contending that she was in the position of a common-law wife. Certainly if she would be able to testify that they had been sexually intimate. As such, she would be a legal heir.

If Ballantine left a will in which Ruth was ignored or given only an insignificant sum, the will could be contested with considerable hope for success, he had said. If Ballantine died intestate — having left no will at all — the chances would be even better, Adamson explained.

But Ballantine had not died intestate. He had made a will while in Fort Worth. She held it in her hand now. What she held was more than just a two-page legal document. It was her very future, the key to the remainder of her life.

She considered the situation for several minutes. It boiled down to two courses of action. The proper thing to do, she knew, was to report discovery of the will to Jamie, and to attorney Adamson, and decide later whether to accept the $5,000.00 bequeathed to her, or to try for what would most certainly be a much larger amount by attempting to establish a common-law marital relationship. Adamson could advise her about this, but that last paragraph of the will almost certainly ruled out any such possibility.

The alternative was simple. Destroy the will and say nothing. Ballantine's note indicated that there was only the one executed and witnessed document. The attorneys in Fort Worth undoubtedly had a copy but if it was not signed and witnessed, it would be of no value in court. After all, John Ballantine could easily have had second thoughts and changed his mind on the way back to Goodland and destroyed the will himself. Who could say otherwise? She knew she would have to say absolutely nothing to anyone, not even to Mr. Adamson.

There was one disadvantage. If she delivered the will to the court and made no attempt to overturn it, she would be certain of $5,000. If she destroyed it, there was a possibility that she would receive nothing at all.

She stood upon the bank of her personal Rubicon. Once the decision was made and implemented, there could be no turning back.

She arose and went to the window at the back of her room. She could see the bunkhouse and workshop. Dr. Black and Dick Thatcher were busy working on the engine of the Packard. A canvas had been spread on the ground and several parts — sparkplugs, she thought likely — were visible.

Beyond the bunkhouse Annie was at work with her hoe in the gardens. "I just can't set around doing nothing, Miss Ruth," she said. "I've got to keep busy at something so I don't think about tomorrow."

Turning, she crossed the hall and went into Jamie's room where the east window looked out toward the lake and Castle Gap. Jamie was sitting at the edge of the lake which was punctuated now and then by the tiny visible but inaudible splash of a pebble she tossed out.

Ruth turned back to her room, the decision made. Moving quickly, she took the will and Ballantine's handwritten note downstairs to the kitchen. On the way, she saw through a window in the living room that Jamie was still sitting on the bank of the lake. Another quick glance out the back door revealed Black, Thatcher and Annie still at their tasks.

Removing the lid from the kitchen range, she saw there were a few hot coals left in the fire box. She crumpled the will and note, thrust them into the stove and touched a match to them. They flared up and were consumed in a few seconds. Taking the poker from behind the stove, Ruth vigorously stirred the ashes until she was satisfied that no one could tell any papers had been burned there.

The deed was done. John Ballantine had died without a will.

Her timing had been most fortunate she realized moments later when she heard an approaching vehicle. She saw a light truck pulling up to the house. Two unfamiliar men got out and came to the front steps. The older of the two introduced himself and his friend. They had been sent by Mr. Sanderson to open the grave for tomorrow's burial.

Jamie was coming from the lake now, and Dr. Black and Thatcher. Together they went to the small burial plot a hundred yards south of the house where Jamie's grandmother had been laid to rest eight years earlier. A simple granite stone marked the grave and was inscribed:

MARGARET BALLANTINE
LOVING WIFE AND MOTHER
1844 — 1904

The plot was carefully tended and enclosed by a white picket fence to keep out roving cattle.

"Jamie," Black said, "your grandfather often referred to Margaret as 'my good right hand.' If you approve, I think it might be appropriate for him to be buried so that she is at his right hand."

The thought brought Jamie close to tears. Without speaking she nodded assent. The two workmen, standing just outside the picket fence, turned to the truck and began unloading their tools. "We understand, Miss Ballantine," the older man said.

Dr. Black returned to the bunkhouse and resumed work on the Packard. "Not much left to do, Dick," he said. "I can finish in a few minutes myself. Appreciate your help earlier."

Ruth went to speak to Annie who had not gone to the burial plot. "It's been a great shock to her," she said to Jamie; "someone needs to visit quietly and reassuringly with her."

Jamie and Dick Thatcher sought the coolness of the east porch. "Jamie I want you to know," Thatcher said as soon as they had taken chairs, "that if there is anything I can do to be of help, you need only to ask. I realize that's the routine thing to say at a time like this but I sincerely mean it. I'm here if you need someone to lean on."

"Thank you. I appreciate it more than you can know. There are things going on here which confuse and disturb me and I've no one to talk to about them unless it be you. I have the feeling that I am going to need a strong friend."

Thatcher got up from his chair, reached out and took her hand, holding it gently between both of his. Surprised, she started to withdraw, but then rose quickly and touched his cheek gently but warmly with her free hand. For a fleeting moment, she felt a surge of emotion that was stronger than anything she had ever known.

Slightly embarrassed, she drew away quickly and sat down in her chair as Thatcher returned to his.

"I'm here whenever you need me, Jamie," he said. "Just whistle. Right now, I think I'd better go back and check on the engine job."

Jamie followed him with her eyes. For better or for worse, an alliance had been formed. Our side against their side. Well, there could be nothing wrong with that, she thought.

It was nearly midnight before sleep finally came to Morgan Black. He had played solitaire in the dining room in the early evening and had gone into the den about 10 o'clock, his usual bedtime. There, stretched out on his cot, he reviewed the situation for the tenth time.

The primary and immediate objective was to have the court appoint him administrator of the Ballantine estate. In that capacity, he would be in reasonably firm control. Since he would be in charge and responsible for expenditures, he could terminate Ruth's and Annie's employment. Thatcher would be no problem. He would simply tell the man to pack up and go.

The girl Jamie was a different story. She had plenty of fire beneath the surface. A stubborn streak, too. If she should decide to live at Bien Escondido, it could constitute a real problem. There was no escaping the fact that he would need the house completely to himself for a minimum of a month, preferably longer.

Well, he thought, he would have to solve that problem when it surfaced. It was always possible that she would leave on her own.

He should have a confidential talk with Judge Oliver in the next few days. The Judge was a close friend, had been for years. More than that, Oliver had expressed a sense of deep personal obligation. In the winter of '96, his young son had been gravely ill with pneumonia. Dr. Black had stayed by the boy's bedside for thirty-six hours without sleep until the crisis had passed. "I owe you more than any man can pay," Oliver had said at the time.

Well, Black thought, now's the time to collect. He would not put the matter crudely. It shouldn't be necessary. He could simply point out that Jamie was the only known relative. That she was young and inexperienced, knew nothing of the conduct of the ranch affairs, or of business in general, for that matter.

And that he, Dr. Black, had been Ballantine's closest confidant for many years and was familiar with his affairs. He could do a much smoother job of closing the estate. Further, he would tell the Judge, he would serve without compensation as administrator because of his long friendship with Ballantine. That ought to about do it, he thought.

Another thing that would require immediate attention was the selection of an attorney for the estate. The selection would have to be made by Jamie since she would be the one to initiate the probate proceedings and this would precede the appointment of an administrator. It was an area where extreme caution must be exercised.

He went over the several possibilities. There were three practicing attorneys in Goodland. James Milliken was probably the best established, best regarded. William Ritchie was new, having been in the county less than a year. Victor Adamson was a very sharp young man. Too sharp, maybe. Ballantine had disliked the man for some reason and the feeling apparently had been mutual.

Since Adamson was definitely out and Ritchie of unknown capability, that left only James Milliken. Jamie would have to be steered to him somehow.

These matters decided, his mind drifted to his son, to the family he had never seen. Now, more strongly than ever, he felt the need to become united with them, to turn over to them the fortune which would soon be his.

CHAPTER 15

Dawn came slowly, reluctantly, to Bien Escondido. The sky hung menacingly low, an inverted bowl that perverse nature had coated with a barely translucent compromise of daylight and darkness. By 9 o'clock a few drops of rain, small and uncertain, began to fall and by 11, a dismal drizzle began which was to last until nightfall.

Not a good day for a burial, Jamie thought, as she looked out her bedroom window toward the lake. Actually, there weren't any good days for burials. They were all bad, some worse than others.

She thought back to her parents' funeral, only six weeks earlier. Spring in Missouri had been in full bloom then. Blossoms were everywhere and their fragrance hinted softly of nature's renewal. Even as the caskets were lowered, a meadowlark had burst into song somewhere above the cemetery.

The Reverend Burkett had called attention in his remarks at the graveside to the scriptural promise of the awakening to a New Life; how the stillness and death of winter are always followed by the resurgence of spring. It would not be so easy today, she thought, and she wondered how the Reverend Jackson, whom she had never met, would handle it.

A little before 11:30, two cars drove up bringing several women from town and Jim and Edith Richardson from their ranch on the

Goodland road. The second car was that of Andrew MacPherson. The women unloaded picnic baskets and carried them to the dining room where the table was prepared for the noon meal.

Of these peopel, Jamie had met only MacPherson. Ruth quickly introduced the others.

The Richardsons apologized. "It's almost sinful that we've not driven over to meet you," Edith Richardson said. "It's only fifteen miles up the road from our place and you've been here two weeks." Jamie murmured what she hoped was an appropriate reply; something about it being warm and reassuring to know that her grandfather's friends had responded when they were most needed.

It seemed to Jamie that Mrs. MacPherson was examining her more intently than the other women. She had no idea why this might be or even if it were actually so, but she had the feeling that Emma MacPherson was measuring her, relating her to some other circumstance or situation. The thought bothered Jamie but she dismissed it.

Following the meal, with more than an hour remaining before the funeral procession was expected from town, the ladies gathered around the dining room table and the men went to the porch where Andrew MacPherson and Jim Richardson exchanged cigars and lighted them.

Going to the porch a few minutes later, Jamie found only MacPherson seated in one of the wicker chairs. Thatcher and Richardson had gotten into a conversation about the history and legends of Castle Gap and the Horsehead Crossing, he explained, and had drifted off in the direction of the lake. "Jim's curious about the pre-Indian culture," MacPherson said. "We all are, I guess.

"On the way out, we met Morgan Black headed for town," he continued. "He'll be back for the services, won't he?"

"Oh, yes," Jamie replied. "Mr. Sanderson asked that he come out with the funeral procession and bring some of the pallbearers."

"I suppose this has come as a considerable shock to Morgan. He and your grandfather were so very close. I've heard a few people in town wonder out loud just what he will do now. This place was more of a home to him than his house in town. He might be interested in buying a part of the ranch after the estate is settled. Not all of it, perhaps, but the portion that includes the buildings and the lake. Has he ever indicated any such interest?"

"I have no idea, Mr. MacPherson. He may have spoken to grandfather but certainly not to me. Anyway, I have no plans for disposition of the ranch and won't be able to even think about it for weeks."

MacPherson did not speak for a few moments, weighing carefully the course he was to follow.

"Miss Jamie," he said in a low voice, "I want to talk to you most confidentially. I feel that as one Missourian to another, we can trust each other. What I am about to say, believe me, is most sincere and meant to be in your best interests."

"Go ahead, Mr. MacPherson. I'll respect your confidence."

"I have a feeling, Jamie, and have had for quite a long time, that your grandfather and Dr. Black shared some sort of secret that was mutually very profitable. Nothing illegal, mind you, but something that common prudence dictated should be conducted in strictest privacy. Now that your grandfather is gone, I think there is a good chance that Morgan Black will try to move very quickly into a position where he can take whatever it is for himself."

"But, Mr. MacPherson, he couldn't really. I'm grandfather's only kin and heir, and whatever he had ought to come to me."

"Normally, yes. Legally, yes. But not everything is done normally and legally, Miss Jamie. Black is capable of cheating you without losing a wink of sleep. Believe me, I know the man."

"You'll have to forgive me, Mr. MacPherson," Jamie said, "but all this is confusing to me. I have no idea what secret grandfather and Dr. Black might have shared, if any. What do you think I should do?"

"Just watch him, Miss Jamie. All of the time. Be alert to any attempt on his part to get you to leave the ranch or to gain control of any situation, especially possession of the house. He'd want that, I'm sure."

"What should I do if I suspect anything like that is developing?"

"Let me know at once and I'll advise you as best I can. There's even a possibility you might be in physical danger here."

"But how could I get in contact with you?" she said. "We've no telephone. Grandfather's Oldsmobile is here but I can't drive. And I certainly can't ask Dr. Black to run me into town so that I can discuss his latest mysterious movements with you."

"There'll be plenty of legitimate reasons for coming to town, Miss Jamie. You will have things to do in connection with John's estate and whenever you are in town you can always find that you need something from the store. Anyway, you're the boss of this spread now and needn't feel it necessary to offer explanations for a trip to town. Transportation shouldn't be any problem. Maybe young Mr. Thatcher can drive John's car. You could even learn to drive it yourself."

It was time, Jamie thought, to end the discussion. Her proper place was in the house with the other ladies and not out on the porch carrying on a confidential conversation with one of the husbands.

"Thanks for your concern, Mr. MacPherson," she said as she

walked toward the door. "I'll be watchful and keep in touch."

Well, she thought, MacPherson is a new dimension to the mystery. That explained, probably, the strange feeling she had about his wife this morning.

The drizzle, which had stopped for a time, began to fall lightly again, bringing Thatcher and Richardson back from their stroll. As they approached, the cars of the funeral procession appeared, headed by Sanderson's new silver-gray motor hearse. The procession continued past the house to the burial plot. In a few moments, those in the house gathered beside the grave, joined by twenty others from town.

The Reverend Jackson was past middle age, a lean and bony type with a long face that might easily have expressed infinite sadness, but fortunately did not. He was totally bald and before he had completed the short opening prayer, tiny rivulets from the increasing drizzle had coursed their way down his face.

The service was brief. Reverend Jackson had apparently been advised by Sanderson as to Ballantine's wishes and he adhered to them. He quoted briefly from Psalms, spoke for two or three minutes on the life John Ballantine had lived, a life beyond reproach, one which could serve as a model for all young men and then finished with another short prayer.

To indicate the conclusion, he turned quickly to Jamie. "Miss Ballantine, please be assured of our deepest sympathy. And now, I think that you and the others should return to the house without delay. I'm sure your grandfather wouldn't want you and his friends standing out here in the rain any longer than necessary."

As Jamie thanked him, he produced a large linen handkerchief and mopped ineffectively at his head. "Could be worse," he said slightly embarrassed. "Could have been snow."

As soon as the little group reached the shelter of the house, the two workmen lowered the casket and quickly began filling the grave. Jamie turned to look back. The sight of two strangers casually and indifferently tossing shovels of sand and gravel down upon her defenseless grandfather was more than she could bear and tears filled her eyes once again. She had not looked back at her parents' graves.

"Please, all of you, come into the dining room," Ruth called from the door. "There are lots of sandwiches and the coffee is hot."

After filling a cup, Sanderson sought out Dr. Black.

"It won't be necessary for you to go back into town, Doctor," he said, "unless you prefer to do so. We can find places in other cars for the pallbearers."

"In that case, I'll stay tonight at the ranch," Black replied. "I've been over the road twice already today."

Thirty minutes later as the group began to break up and move toward the cars, Dick Thatcher spoke briefly to Andrew MacPherson. "Could I ask a small favor, Mr. MacPherson? Would it be too much trouble for you to mail a letter for me?"

"No problem or trouble at all," MacPherson replied. "Won't be time this afternoon but since there aren't any trains tonight, tomorrow morning will be just as good. I go to the postoffice every morning at 8 o'clock and I'll mail it then."

"I'll really appreciate it, Mr. MacPherson. I had the letter with me when we came in to town to meet Mr. Ballantine's train, but things happened so rapidly I just didn't get it to the post office."

By 4 o'clock Sanderson's two workmen, who had followed the funeral procession from town at a discreet distance and had then parked their light truck near the bunkhouse, had finished filling the grave and shaping the mound. When they left, Black and Thatcher, who had been watching silently from the porch, went into the house where Dr. Black cleared his throat and asked for attention.

"Miss Jamie," he began, "I believe tomorrow would not be too soon for you to begin to address the matters that will need attention. No necessity for any specific action at the moment except for two things. First, you should decide on an attorney to handle the closing of your grandfather's estate. Second, you will need to make a search for a will. It's true that John told me only a few days ago that he had no will and I see no reason to doubt this. However, he did consult his attorneys in Fort Worth about ranch leases I think, and there is the outside possibility that he could have talked to them about a will, also."

"Couldn't the attorney we select, whoever he may be, get in touch with the Fort Worth lawyers and find out?" Jamie asked.

"Yes, of course," Black said. "But probably the first question the local attorney will ask is whether or not you have made a search here. Your grandfather did not have a safe deposit box in Goodland, Miss Jamie. He told me that. You can verify this at the bank. His ranch leases and other papers he considered important are kept in a metal box in the wardrobe in his room.

"Also," he continued, "if he had made a will in Forth Worth, it should have been in his possession when he collapsed on the train."

"I'm afraid there was nothing, Doctor," Ruth said. "I unpacked his suitcase yesterday afternoon — he had only the one — and put his things away. There was a page of handwritten notes about proposed changes in the ranch lease arrangements which I put in the drawer of the desk in his room. But there were no other papers. Certainly there was no will. Mr. Sanderson gave us the items John had on his person. You were present at the funeral parlor. I believe I recall that he said specifically there were no papers of any kind."

"Yes, he did say that," Black replied. "Do you know anything about the metal box in his room?"

"I've seen it, of course, many times," Ruth said. "But I have no idea what might be in it. John never mentioned it and I did not consider it my business to ask."

"Let's start there, then," Black said. He moved toward the stairs, Jamie and Ruth following.

The box was quickly located but found to be locked. Jamie went to her room and returned with Ballantine's key ring which Sanderson had given her. A small, thin key fit the lock and the contents of the box were soon spread out on the bed.

There were several recorded land deeds, some abstracts of title, tax receipts, the current ranch leases and a couple of expired leases. There was also a handwritten note which had been placed on top of everything else, where it could be immediately found:

TO WHOM IT MAY CONCERN: In the event of my death, please keep any services very brief and lay me to rest beside my dear wife here on the ranch. I would like my old friend, Morgan Black, to administer my estate. I have left no will and my property therefore will descend to my legal heirs according to the laws of the State of Texas. John B. Ballantine.

"That would appear to settle the matter of a will," Black said. "In order to assure the court, however, I believe John's room should be checked out carefully. In the meantime I will look through the den, although I am certain nothing is there. John did keep his business records pertaining to the ranch operations in a file in the den. Also his business and personal correspondence but not much of anything else. In the light of his note, I'm sure there will be no will in the den."

Thirty minutes later Jamie and Ruth returned to the living room where Dr. Black was already waiting. Nothing had been found.

"I believe I should keep John's note from the lockbox since it makes specific reference to me," Black said. "I'll deliver it to the attorney you select, Miss Jamie. And that brings us to the second thing. An attorney for the estate should be chosen this evening."

Thatcher rose to his fee saying he felt it would be inappropriate if he were present during the discussion. "I'll just loaf around the bunkhouse for an hour or so until suppertime," he said and left the room.

They were all silent for a few moments. Then Ruth spoke.

"If I may make a suggestion, Jamie, I think that you should not consider Victor Adamson. John disliked him. Your grandfather would not rest easily, I'm afraid, if he knew that Victor Adamson were in charge of his estate."

"I agree," Black said quickly. "Adamson wouldn't do at all. And that man, Bill Ritchie, is young and inexperienced. A nice enough sort, I guess, but I couldn't feel confidence in him."

"So where does that leave us?" Jamie asked.

"It leaves us with the man who is probably the most experienced and best qualified — James Milliken," Black replied.

It was all happening too fast, Jamie thought, and she could not avoid the feeling of being manipulated. It occurred to her that she should postpone the decision for a day or so, but she decided that nothing would be gained. "I guess Mr. Milliken it is, then," she said. "We should go to town tomorrow to get things in motion, I suppose."

After a light supper with little conversation, Dr. Black retired to the den. He had some reading, he said, which would last until bedtime. Jamie and Thatcher went to the porch.

"A day or two ago, Dick, you asked about staying on and continuing your work," Jamie said. "Yesterday you said you wanted to do anything you could in order to help me."

"I sincerely meant it, Jamie," Thatcher said.

"Then you can help me most by staying here and going on with your explorations just as if nothing had happened to grandfather. I guess I'm in charge now, more or less, and entitled to extend that invitation. I may call on you for your help, soon and often."

She rose from her chair and turned to the door. Thatcher moved quickly to stand beside her for a brief moment before she entered the house. He touched her cheek gently, fleetingly, and received a warm smile in return.

Andrew MacPherson had returned to Goodland without participating in the conversation in the back seat, occupied by Emma, the Reverend Jackson's wife Pearl and a Mrs. Riley. He couldn't hear what was being said over the wind and the sound of the tires and was secretly please that he could not. His mind was on other matters.

When their passengers had been delivered and they had reached the privacy of their home, they sat facing each other over the kitchen table. MacPherson described his confidential talk with Jamie.

"I guess I acted on the spur of the moment, Emma," he said. "I believe, however, that I have gotten the girl's confidence and planted suspicion of Black in her mind. If I'm correct, Morgan Black will make every possible effort, legal or not, to get Jamie Ballantine out of his way. After that, whatever he and John secretly shared would be his alone. If he fails to deal with Jamie successfully, he could lose out completely and I'm convinced more than ever that what is involved is of very substantial value and he will want it all."

"How should we proceed now?" Emma asked. "Should you go on with your plan to have your San Antonio friend shadow Dr. Black the next time he goes there?"

"I think not. John Ballantine's death has changed everything. I think we must align ourselves with Jamie, at least in appearance, in an effort to find out just what we are dealing with. The girl is young and inexperienced and might confide in me if she should become frightened. But we should be prepared to go over to Black's side if it seems advisable. We must be flexible. As before, if we can get to the bottom of this, our silence would be our price for a share of the action."

Both were quiet for a few moments.

"There's another thing, Emma. This afternoon Thatcher gave me a letter to mail. It's addressed to someone in Dallas. Apparently it was written before Ballantine's death. Thatcher said that in the confusion at the station he forgot to mail it."

"Probably it's just a letter to a friend about what he's doing here."

"That's the point, Emma. What's he doing here? I have an uneasy feeling that this amateur archaeology business is only a cover for something else. I've never done anything like this before but I suggest we find out what's in the letter."

Emma said nothing. Then, she took the letter which her husband had placed on the table. A thin wisp of steam was coming from the teakettle on the kitchen range and she held the envelope in it until the glue softened, then removed the letter and placed it on the table.

"I've done my part," she said.

MacPherson unfolded the letter and read it silently, then aloud. "Nothing about pre-Indian culture," he said. "Just about Morgan Black and, for some reason, Morgan's father who once lived in Denton. It doesn't help solve any mystery. Just complicates it. Now, we'll have to keep an eye on Thatcher as well as Black and Jamie Ballantine."

The envelope was carefully resealed. Just before going to bed, MacPherson examined it. The flap was perfectly dry, sealed tightly and there was no evidence that it had been opened.

Jamie's diary entry that night was brief.

Bien Escondido, May 31.

We buried grandfather today next to grandmother in the family plot. It was a rainy, gloomy day, but quite a number of people came all the way from town for the burial. Grandfather had lots of friends here, I guess.

> *Something strange happened this afternoon following
> the graveside service. Mr. MacPherson, the owner of the
> general store in town, spoke to me very confidentially. He
> wanted to warn me about Dr. Black. Said that Black was
> after something that had been shared with grandfather and
> that I probably stood in the way. My physical safety was
> even involved, he said.*
>
> *It was kind of him to caution me, I'm sure. But is he just
> concerned about me, or does he have some ulterior motive?
> Can I trust Andrew MacPherson? Can I trust anybody at all?
> Certainly not Ruth Hazelton. Not Morgan Black, whose
> sincerity I have suspected from the beginning. Insane as the
> thought may be, the only one I'm confident of is a man I
> have know for less than a week. Dick Thatcher.*

She returned the diary to its hiding place and rearranged her
mousetrap. Tomorrow, she thought, things would begin to happen
when they went to arrange for probate of the estate. And Morgan Black
would begin to realize that Jamie Ballantine was not an adversary to be
dismissed — but the boss of Bien Escondido.

CHAPTER 16

"I think we should go to town first thing this morning, Jamie,"
Black said as the breakfast dishes were being cleared. "Hopefully, we
can see Milliken, but if he should have other appointments or court
hearings, we could arrange to meet with him in the afternoon."

"I'll be ready in fifteen minutes, Doctor," Jamie said.

Black turned to Ruth. "Do you want to go in with us, Ruth?"

"Yes, I do," Ruth said. "There are three or four things I want to do.
I'll be ready when Jamie is."

"How about you, Thatcher?"

"Thanks but I'll stay here today. I plan to check out the area south
of the old trail and east of the lake. Then tomorrow, I'll work to the
north of the trail. That'll about do for the preliminary reconnaissance."

In Goodland, Ruth was let out at Virginia Dolan's shop. She visited briefly with Mrs. Dolan, then went directly to the law office of Victor Adamson, a small second-floor suite on Main street.

"I've been expecting you, Mrs. Hazelton," Adamson said, "although not quite this soon."

"I see no reason for delay, Mr. Adamson. Nothing is going to change. Jamie Ballantine and Dr. Black are at Milliken's office right now. Jamie plans to ask him to serve as attorney for John's estate. This was Morgan Black's recommendation and he seems to be more or less running things, or at least trying to."

"Do you want me to represent you? Along the lines we discussed previously?"

"I do, Mr. Adamson. I understand what will be necessary and I am prepared to testify to any extent necessary."

"What will be necessary, Mrs. Hazelton, is for you to testify under oath that you were physically intimate with John Ballantine. Not just once but on a regular basis, that you fulfilled the normal conjugal duties of a wife. And this would have to be willingly, voluntarily. You should testify that you were acting on his suggestion or invitation. Can you do this?"

"Yes, Mr. Adamson, I can and will."

"All right. Now, do you know if John left a will?"

Ruth hesitated. It was the question she had feared.

"I believe he did not, Mr. Adamson," she said in a level voice. "We searched carefully and found nothing. There was a note in his handwriting in the lockbox where he kept his leases and title papers. The note said that he had made no will and asked that Dr. Black be made administrator of his estate. Black has the note. He said it would be appropriate for him to have it since he was specifically mentioned."

"Was the note dated?"

Ruth thought a moment. "I'm not certain," she said, "but I think not."

"All right, Ruth. Here's how we will proceed. We'll let Jamie Ballantine petition the probate court through her attorney Milliken for administration of the estate. The court will appoint an administrator and will set a date for the filing of claims and get things in motion. I understand Jamie is the only living blood relative of John Ballantine and I suppose her petition will allege this and ask that the court so find.

"At an appropriate time I'll file a petition on your behalf asking that the court recognize your status as the common-law wife of John Ballantine and that in the absence of a will, his property should descend as provided by the statutes of the state governing intestate decedents.

If the court so finds, then you and Jamie would share the inheritance."

"Is there anything I should do now?" Ruth asked.

"Nothing. Go on just as if you had not talked to me. Just let me handle things at the appropriate time. There will be plenty of fireworks as soon as your petition is filed.

"One thing. Perhaps you should think of a place to stay in town. I imagine you will be asked to leave the ranch when the storm breaks."

Ruth left Adamson's office with a feeling of satisfaction. She had handled the risky matter of Ballantine's will calmly and, having crossed that bridge, she felt confident of her ability to carry it off.

At James Milliken's office, Black asked Jamie to wait in the outer office while he talked briefly to Milliken. It was with reference to some personal business of his, he said, entirely unrelated to the Ballantine estate matter, and would take only five minutes.

"What can I do for you, Morgan?" Milliken asked closing the door.

"I have Miss Jamie Ballantine with me. She's waiting in the outer office. We are here to ask you to serve as attorney in the closing of the Ballantine estate. I felt it might be advisable for me to visit personally, and confidentially, with you in advance. I would prefer that she not know about this conversation.

"You see, I believe John left no will. He did indicate to me verbally before his death that he would like to have me serve as administrator of his estate should he die before I did. And he left a note in his handwriting to the same effect."

"I see no problem, Morgan," Milliken said. "Having known the two of you for years, I know John would have wanted that. And I know you to be capable and conscientious. I'm sure the judge will agree."

"Thanks, Jim. But there is a problem. Miss Ballantine is strongwilled and I have the feeling she may wish to be appointed herself. Nothing wrong, I suppose, except she is totally inexperienced, knows nothing about the ranch operation and is not even a citizen of Texas, if that makes any difference. And it would be completely contrary to her grandfather's wishes."

"You've raised an interesting legal point concerning residence in Texas, Morgan. I can't recall that it has come up before in my experience. I rather think the statutes are silent on the matter although there might be some case law. I could look into it but it may not be necessary. I'm in agreement with the other points you make and feel the estate would be better served with you handling it. I will so advise her. That may be sufficient. You can bring her in now."

Milliken began as soon as Jamie was seated at the heavy oak conference table. "Miss Ballantine, Dr. Black says you wish to confer with me concerning your grandfather's estate."

"Yes, Mr. Milliken, I do. We have discussed this and want to retain you as attorney for the estate."

"Very well, Miss Jamie. May I call you that?"

"Yes, please do."

"All right, then. It is usually advisable to get a probate started as quickly as possible so that someone is empowered to act; to pay bills and do other necessary things. I will prepare the petition tomorrow but will need certain information. You are John Ballantine's granddaughter, are you not?"

"Yes. I am, in fact, his only living blood relative. I have no brothers or sisters and both of my parents were killed in an automobile accident in Missouri a few weeks ago."

"Yes, I heard, Miss Jamie, I'm sorry."

"My father was an only child, too, so that I have no Ballantine uncles, aunts or cousins. Nor any on my mother's side, either. Mother had only one sister and she died long ago without having been married. So you see, grandfather was all I had and I was all he had."

"Your grandfather had no other living relatives at all?"

"No, Mr. Milliken. He had one brother who was killed at Gettysburg. He was with General Pickett. The brother was only nineteen and not married. And my grandmother, as you know, died in 1904."

Milliken thought a moment. "Well," he said, "I believe you have covered all the bases. Assuming these facts are correct, and I do not doubt them, it would appear you are the sole heir to the Ballantine estate. As such, you would certainly be entitled to petition the court for probate. Now do you know if your grandfather made a will?"

"We have not been able to locate one, Mr. Milliken. We did find a handwritten note which I think Dr. Black has with him."

Black produced the note without comment and handed it to the attorney. "It isn't dated as you may have observed," Milliken said. "It could have been written only the day before John boarded the train to Fort Worth or it might have been two or three years earlier. Probably no way of knowing. I'll check with the other attorneys in town. If they tell me they did not prepare a will for John, and if nothing has been filed with the probate court, we'll have to assume he died intestate."

"There is one other thing, though," Jamie said. "Grandfather planned to see his attorneys in Fort Worth when he was there last week about ranch leases. I don't know if he could have done anything about a will then or not. Shouldn't you check with them, too?"

"Yes, of course. I can and will. I know the firm. Now, the only other thing to be settled today is appointment of an administrator, or an executor in case a will turns up. The note left by your grandfather asks that Dr. Black be appointed to serve. Would you have any objection to that, Miss Jamie?"

Jamie thought a long moment before answering.

"Is there any reason why . . . why I could not serve in that capacity, Mr. Milliken?"

"It is possible that you might not qualify because you are not a resident. Technically, you are only a visitor in this state and county. I would have to study the matter. However, there are other reasons which I consider significant. Because of his long friendship and association with your grandfather, Dr. Black is very familiar with the ranch operations and probably other business interests John Ballantine may have had. Also, if I may say, you are young and inexperienced."

"I may be young, Mr. Milliken, but I am not inexperienced. I was appointed administratrix of my father's estate in Missouri. In fact, I have not yet been discharged in that capacity. There was very little to administer, really. It has been mostly a matter of turning things over to the creditors to satisfy their claims. Nevertheless, I imagine procedures in this state are similar to those in Missouri."

"Basically, yes," Milliken replied. "However, there is a very large difference in scope. From what you say, I imagine your father's estate was quite small. Your grandfather's will be relatively large and may be somewhat complex. Further, I am not certain that you can, or should, serve in an administrative capacity in two estates of your immediate family at the same time. I feel sure the judge would look unfavorably on that aspect. In view of these several factors, I cannot in good conscience recommend that you petition the court for your appointment. You have retained me to advise you and my advice is that you ask for appointment of Morgan Black. Assuming that he is willing to serve."

"Yes, of course, Jim" Black said. "I'll do so for two reasons. First, you have advised it and I respect your judgment. Second, it was John's request that I do so and he was as close to me as if we were brothers. And one more thing, Jim — and Miss Jamie — I'll serve without the usual compensation allowed an administrator out of respect for John."

The walls were closing in upon her. She had been in the attorney's office only a few minutes and already Milliken and Black had apparently formed an alliance against her. It wasn't fair, she thought. Two mature and experienced men against a lone girl, and from what they said, the probate judge would probably side with them, too.

"All right, Mr. Milliken," she said aloud. "Please have the petition ask for Dr. Black as administrator."

To herself she thought, *just because you have won this initial skirmish, Doctor, doesn't mean you've won the battle.* She would see how things worked out and if Morgan Black tried to lean too heavily on her she could fire Milliken, get another attorney for the estate and ask the court to replace Black.

After making arrangements for Jamie to come to town two days later to review and sign the petition, they left the law office, picked up Ruth Hazelton and returned to the ranch.

CHAPTER 17

"I don't think you should, Jamie," Ruth said. "Think carefully before you go."

"Why do you feel I shouldn't?" Jamie asked.

Ruth turned her eyes to the floor. "It's just that...well, it's something a nice girl would not do if she values her reputation. She just does not go traipsing off into the brush for an entire day with a man she scarcely knows."

Jamie bristled. "That's a term I have always disliked. Particularly when the correct meaning of the word 'nice' is so far removed from common interpretation. As far as I am concerned, I am a 'nice' girl as you define the word. And whether it does or does not damage my reputation, I am going to spend the day with Dick Thatcher."

Without replying Ruth turned and left Jamie's room, going all the way downstairs and out into the yard. Jamie resumed the lacing of her hiking boots. How quickly, she thought, Ruth had averted her eyes when the matter of danger in the brush had been mentioned. Her guilt was obvious.

Morgan Black had left the ranch immediately after breakfast saying that he would go in to the bank and verify that Ballantine did not have a safe deposit box or papers left at the bank for safekeeping. Although he had made no mention of it, he planned also to call on Judge Oliver and smooth the way for his appointment as administrator.

He would ask the judge to move things along as quickly as possible. There would be, he knew, a necessary delay of three weeks or so before a formal hearing could be had, following which letters of administration could be issued to him. In the meantime he would not need to remain idle. There was a good possibility, he thought, that he might be able to persuade Jamie to return to Missouri, and Ruth and Annie to quit work and leave Bien Escondido. Certainly it would be preferable if they did these things voluntarily rather than under pressure from him as administrator. There would be no reason for Jamie to remain in Texas once the administration was under way. She could return in the fall when they were ready to wind things up. He would suggest that Dick Thatcher leave and if the man did not do so graciously, he would have to be sent away less politely.

He felt things were going well. Jamie had made a brief show of resistance in Milliken's office but had folded up rather quickly. Not as strong-willed as he had thought.

By noon Jamie and Dick had searched back and forth across a rectangular area two miles square and had stopped for lunch in a small patch of shade on the lake's east bank. There was a thin cover of grass and two or three scraggly trees offered partial protection from the sun. Jamie spread a cloth and removed the water canteen, two glasses and several sandwiches from her knapsack.

"I suppose," Dick said between bites, "that it was forward of me, presumptuous perhaps, to ask you to come along today. Did you get any reaction?"

"Only from Ruth, which I expected. I could see the wheels going around in Morgan Black's head but he didn't say anything. He was thinking something, I'm sure, but I very much doubt if it concerned my social conduct."

"I can't tell you how grateful I am, Jamie, for your permitting me to stay on. I had made plans for this trip for more than a year and having to cancel things would have been a big disappointment."

"Your leaving Bien Escondido would be much more than a disappointment for me, Dick. I would have to pack up and go back to Missouri or somewhere. Frankly, I'd be afraid to stay here. I'm not easily frightened, but I'm just a little scared right now."

"Do you want to tell me about it?"

"Yes. Yes, I believe so. You're the only one I can trust.

"I might as well start with Andrew McPherson. You met him. He has the general store in town. On the afternoon of grandfather's funeral he spoke to me privately and in confidence. He said I might be in physical danger and named Morgan Black as the source."

"Did he say why?"

"He believes grandfather and Dr. Black shared some sort of secret, somehow connected to the ranch which had been highly profitable to both of them. Now that grandfather was gone, Mr. MacPherson said, he believed Black would want everything for himself, whatever it was or is. And that I stood in the way and must somehow be gotten rid of."

"Do you think Dr. Black would resort to violence?"

"I think not. His manner is more subtle. He wants to be appointed administrator of grandfather's estate and then take physical possession of the ranch — and I mean move right into the house — in order to discharge his administrative duties. I'm sure he plans to let both Ruth and Annie go and under those conditions it would not be socially acceptable for me to stay on in the house. I'd be scared to, anyway. Somewhere along the way he would terminate your invitation too so he would have the place entirely to himself. Why this is necessary I don't know, but I'm certain that is his plan."

"Can't you block his appointment? Get yourself appointed instead?"

"I doubt it. The attorney we retained said that since I am technically not a citizen of this state, I couldn't qualify. Anyway the petition to the probate court is going to ask for Dr. Black's appointment. I go in tomorrow to sign it. Somehow it seemed there was nothing else I could do."

Thatcher was silent for a moment. "I'm wondering about MacPherson. Do you suppose he could harbor some sort of grudge against Black? Or maybe just have an over-active imagination?"

"I think not, Dick. There are too many other things. I made up my mind several days ago that there was some sort of conspiracy between my grandfather and the doctor. Something that paid off for both of them. Everything points that way. Dr. Black has spent almost no time in the active practice of medicine for years yet he lives very well. My grandfather has not operated the ranch as a going concern for ages, yet he also lived well. Between the two they arranged that at least one of them was at the ranch almost all of the time as if guarding something."

"And you have no idea what?"

"None at all, Dick, except that the location of the ranch and the main house itself has something to do with it. Grandfather fibbed to me I'm sorry to say, right after I came out. I wondered why he had selected such a desolate location. He said he hoped the railroad would come through Castle Gap and across his land making it much more valuable. But I learned later that the railroad right-of-way had been purchased two years earlier, far to the north, and that it was common knowledge."

"Well," Thatcher said, "it would seem Dr. Black wants everybody out of the way so he can have a free hand to secretly dispose of whatever it was your grandfather started with him — cutting you out in the process. I don't think he wants to harm you, just to get you away from Bien Escondido."

"He's not the only one who wants me gone." Jamie related the events of the arrowhead-hunting expedition that Ruth had turned into a confrontation with terror. As the memory of those frightening moments returned, she began to sob. Thatcher moved quickly to her side, pulled her to her feet and took her warmly into his arms. He kissed her forehead, her ear and finally her lips.

She felt herself responding spontaneously, almost fiercely. Her eagerness was at once surprising and pleasing to her.

"What has happened to you is more than any girl should have to take," she heard him saying. "Things are going to be different for you," he said as he released her. "Believe me, Jamie, they will be."

They gathered up the remnants of the lunch and started back. As they reached the arroyo at the north end of the lake, Jamie stopped.

"There's one other thing I ought to mention," she said. "Bien Escondido. The name of this place. Somehow, I feel it was grandfather's private joke on the world. Something is surely 'well hidden' here, but it is not the ranch or the ranch house. Both of them are as obvious as can be. Whatever it is, it has great value and is responsible for the strange actions of both grandfather and Dr. Black. Maybe Ruth's too."

Jamie paused a moment and then looked directly into Thatcher's eyes. "I have been open and honest with you, Dick," she said in a level voice. "I've told you everything, held back nothing. Now it's time for you to be frank with me."

"What is it you want to know?"

"Just this, Dick. Forgive me if I am being too direct, but you aren't an archaeologist at all, are you? Not even an amateur one. It's a screen for something else, isn't it?"

Thatcher took her hands and held them with obvious affection.

"I guess I'm not a very good actor, Jamie," he said, smiling. "The whole idea of a search for pre-Indian culture was just a little preposterous. I sensed that Dr. Black has had doubts about me all along."

Jamie thought a moment. "Tell me about it when you're ready."

"For now, Jamie," Thatcher said, "two things. First, you were right about your grandfather and Dr. Black sharing a valuable secret. I propose that we step in, as full partners, and take over. Is that agreeable?"

Jamie nodded assent. "And what is the second thing?"

"The second thing, Jamie, has to do with your remark a few minutes ago. You said that your grandfather and Black were guarding something. I know what it is."

CHAPTER 18

The following day Jamie and Morgan Black met with attorney Milliken in his office at 2 p.m. The petition to the probate court had been prepared. Jamie read it carefully, then signed it.

"I'll file it this afternoon, Miss Jamie," Milliken said. "Judge Oliver will issue an order for a hearing on the matter immediately. The hearing will probably be June 24 or 25 and, assuming there are no other filings or unforeseen delays, the order appointing Dr. Black will be issued that same day. In the meantime, if you need any temporary funds before Morgan is qualified to act, we can make arrangements."

"I don't think that will be necessary, Mr. Milliken. I have a modest amount of cash and the Ballantine credit is good for whatever necessities we might need I am sure."

After leaving the office, Jamie asked to be let out at MacPherson's store with the explanation that she wished to purchase several packets of flower seed to sow on her grandfather's grave. "It's about all I can do as a memorial," she said, "until we can have a permanent stone set."

Black agreed and said he would go over to the garage and have the Packard's gas tank filled and buy a new spark plug. He and Thatcher had found one that had a crack in the porcelain, he said.

"I'll be back for you in twenty minutes," he said, as Jamie stepped into the shade of the MacPherson awning.

After purchasing her flower seeds Jamie sought out MacPherson. He greeted her warmly and offered her a chair.

"Anything to report?" he said.

"I suppose it would be accurate to say," Jamie replied, "that hostilities are about to start. I signed the probate petition this afternoon and Dr. Black will no doubt be appointed in about three weeks. I suspect that he will not wait that long to put on the pressure. I predict that he will, within a week, begin making suggestions to get me away from the ranch. Ruth, too."

MacPherson thought carefully before replying. "I'm not sure how I should advise you," he said after a moment. "It would be best if you could stay on at the ranch and keep him from having an entirely free hand. At the same time, it might not be safe for you to do so."

Jamie waited for MacPherson to continue. Finally he spoke.

"I'm going to make a suggestion, Miss Jamie, that you may not welcome. I think we are in agreement that something of very substantial value is involved and that Dr. Black will do anything possible to keep you from having your grandfather's share of it. It seems to me you are alone and outnumbered. I would like to come in on your side, but frankly, if I do, I would expect you to share with me, only modestly, but nevertheless to a reasonable extent. We could work out details later, of course. Can I offer my help on such a basis?"

"Let me think about it for a few days, Mr. MacPherson. I appreciate your offer of help. But I'd still like a little time."

To herself she thought, *at least I know where he stands. He's on somebody's side, no question about it — MacPherson's.*

"One thing more," MacPherson said. "You mentioned that your grandfather had shown you a spot near the north end of the lake where he had found rusted and burned wagon irons years ago. No trace of them remains now, I understand. I am almost one hundred percent certain that those wagon irons were the starting point of the mystery of Bien Escondido and perhaps the key to solving that mystery."

"Perhaps, Mr. MacPherson. I have told you everything I know about that. Grandfather mentioned it only the one time. But now I think I should go. The doctor will probably be waiting outside. I'll think on your suggestion and visit you next week."

The drive back to the ranch was accomplished without conversation but as the Packard stopped at the front steps, Black asked Jamie to wait a moment before leaving the car.

"I'd appreciate it, Miss Jamie," he said, "if you would ask Ruth and Annie to join you in the living room. There are a few things we must discuss and I see no point in waiting. If Mr. Thatcher is around, he should be asked to leave the house until our conversation is concluded. It will not be a matter for his proper concern."

Jamie did not answer but stepped down from the car and went into the house. It was happening sooner than she had anticipated, she thought. But she was as well prepared now as she would be next week, she felt, for whatever challenge Black chose to throw at her.

At Jamie's request, Ruth and Annie came into the living room and were joined by Dr. Black. Dick Thatcher was nowhere to be seen.

"What I have to say," Black began, "concerns all three of you. Since it's not an easy thing for me to do, I would like to get it over with as quickly as possible.

"First, I do not plan to continue with your employment, Ruth — or Annie's — after my appointment as administrator becomes effective.

There will be no need for your services and the wages would therefore be an improper use of estate funds, the expenditure of which is my sole responsibility. I must account for and justify such expenditures in my report to the court. It seems to be only fair to let both of you know now so you can make arrangements to leave without having this thrown at you unexpectedly in two or three weeks.

"And Miss Jamie, it would be extremely inappropriate for you to stay on by yourself — a young woman alone in a rough country with the nearest neighbor more than a dozen miles away. I would urge you to return to Missouri at the same time Ruth and Annie leave. The administration of your grandfather's estate will not require your presence until perhaps early autumn. In the meantime you can enjoy the companionship of your old friends and see to the conclusion of your father's estate. You can return when I send for you."

Ruth was the first to speak. "If I understand you correctly, doctor, you are suggesting that all three of us leave Bien Escondido as soon as possible. Who, may I ask, is going to take care of this house?"

"I will, Ruth," Black replied. "I might just as well 'batch' out here as in town. I've been doing it and getting along very well for fifty years or so. And it's not a lifetime sentence to my own cooking, you know. Two or three months at the most. By then the estate work will be completed and Jamie will be in a position to do whatever she wishes with the ranch property. You understand that, don't you, Jamie?"

"Frankly, doctor, I'm not sure I do," Jamie replied. "One thing I am sure of though. You haven't bothered to ask my opinion or to inquire into my wishes in the matter. I want, and plan, to stay here on the ranch all summer and I expect to have Ruth and Annie with me."

Morgan Black's eyes visibly narrowed, his lips compressed into a thin, tight line. He rose from his chair, walked to the end of the room and stood for a long moment, contemplating the massive set of elk antlers mounted above the fireplace. Then he turned and spoke.

"I cannot countenance, and will not permit, any payment of wages for Ruth and Annie from estate funds. Further, I will be forced to ask the court for an order requiring them to vacate these premises if they do not do so voluntarily."

"As far as payment is concerned, doctor," Jamie replied, "you will not need to give any thought to it. I will pay their wages from my own funds. All I need to do is open an account at the Cattleman's Bank in town and instruct my bank in Missouri to transfer funds here. And as to an order requiring them to leave, I very much doubt if your authority as administrator will stretch that far. As grandfather's sole heir, I am in physical possession of Bien Escondido and I intend to remain in possession, and that includes determining who shall occupy this house. Including Mr. Thatcher, if I should decide to ask him to stay."

"You are making a serious mistake, Miss Jamie, and one which I believe you will regret."

"I think not, doctor. And while we're on the subject of who is in charge, I ask that you turn over to me the key to grandfather's den."

"That," Black replied, "I will not do. All of the business records pertaining to the ranch — matters pertinent to the administration of the estate — are in that room. I intend to see that they remain undisturbed until I am officially empowered to act. Your grandfather entrusted me with that key and I do not intend to violate that trust, tonight or ever."

It was obvious to Jamie from the rigid set of Black's jaw that he was not going to back down. Perhaps she should settle for a small gain. "Would you have any objection, Dr. Black, to opening the door so that I can at least see the interior of the room? Surely that can't do any harm to the business records and it's the least I am entitled to."

Without speaking, Black crossed the room and unlocked the door. Jamie came and stood in the doorway without attempting to enter.

The room was smaller than her upstairs bedroom and contained a large desk with matching chair, a filing cabinet, two occasional chairs, a hatrack and the cot occupied by Dr. Black when staying overnight. An ornamental kerosene lamp stood on one corner of the desk, a cigar humidor on another, and several newspapers and magazines were neatly stacked in the center. The wall to the left of the door supported a hardwood gun rack carrying what appeared to Jamie to be two lever-action hunting rifles and two shotguns. On the opposite wall her grandfather had hung a large, framed lithograph of Custer's Last Stand. A heavy, brown broadloom carpet covered the floor.

"Are you satisfied, Miss Jamie?" Black asked after a few moments. "What you have seen is of course exactly what you might expect to see in any western gentleman's den or private office. The business records are in the desk drawers and the filing cabinet and as I have already told you I intend that they shall stay there until I am discharged as administrator."

"Thank you, doctor," Jamie said, and turned away from the door. Black went in, closed the door and turned the key in the lock.

"Well, let him brood," Jamie said, addressing both Ruth and Annie as they returned to the living room. "At least the air is cleared. We know where he stands and he knows where I stand. And I hope that both of you will stand fast with me."

"Jamie," Ruth said, "I'm sorry but I am not at all certain as to what

I should do. I don't want to be the cause of any trouble between you and Morgan or any other kind of a problem. Maybe it would be better if I took his advice and left. Let me sleep on it and tell you tomorrow."

"All right, Ruth. And how about you, Annie?"

"I'll stay on a while, Miss Jamie," Annie said. "It's not that I couldn't get a job somewhere else. It wouldn't be no big problem. But I'm used to this place and I like you. If you want me to stay, I will."

Almost as if by mutual consent there was no supper, at least in the normal sense. Dr. Black did not emerge from the den and no one made any effort to call him. Ruth announced that she was too upset by the afternoon's developments to eat anything and went to her room. Annie foraged for herself in the kitchen.

Around 6:30, Thatcher appeared from the arroyo just north of the lake carrying a spade and shovel. Jamie watched as he crossed the ranch yard, went to the tool shed and replaced the spade and shovel, and continued on to the bunkhouse. She quickly prepared two large sandwiches and took them to the foreman's room.

"Room service!" she said as Thatcher opened the door in response to her knock. "Supper is definitely not being served in the main dining room at Bien Escondido this evening, so I brought you these."

Thatcher listened with careful attention as Jamie described her confrontation with Dr. Black. Now and then he nodded approval as her temper flared anew with the description of Black's arrogance.

"You handled it exactly right and I'm proud of you," he said. "If you had backed down or shown any sign of weakness he would have been in charge from that moment on. If you hadn't faced up to him, I'm sure that both Ruth and Annie would have made plans to leave immediately and you would have been forced to go also."

"Annie's going to stay with me but I'm not sure about Ruth," Jamie said. "She is to let me know in the morning. Frankly, if she goes, I won't miss her. At least I won't have to look for rattlesnakes between the sheets every night. I'm going back to the house now. Enjoy your sandwiches. We'll talk more tomorrow."

As she left, Thatcher placed a reassuring hand on her shoulder and she brushed his cheek gently with a quick kiss.

Late that night in the quiet of her bedroom, Ruth Hazelton sat in deep thought. Things were moving rapidly and everyone's cards were being laid on the table. Everyone's except hers, of course. That development could occur when Victor Adamson filed his petition asking the court to find Ruth to be John Ballantine's common-law wife and heir. It would be best to be gone from the ranch when that happened, she thought, and fortunately Dr. Black had made that possible.

And there was something involved that was much more than just ownership of several thousand arid acres and a set of ranch buildings. She had known that for three or four years. Whatever it was, it could be of greater value than the ranch and all John Ballantine's visible assets, she felt, and it made Morgan Black as much her opponent as Jamie.

She made her decision. She would leave Bien Escondido tomorrow.

CHAPTER 19

The following morning immediately after breakfast, Ruth called Jamie aside. "I don't want you to think I am unappreciative of your offer, Jamie," she said, "but all things considered it is probably best that I do as Morgan suggests. I've been wanting to visit what family I have left in Little Rock and now might be the time to do just that, especially with the heat and dust of July and August coming up."

"Will you go to Arkansas right away?" Jamie asked.

"Not immediately. I plan to take a room at the Texan temporarily. I'll have to write my cousins and let them know I'm coming. It wouldn't do to show up without notice. In the meantime, I have a few odds and ends to do in town. Mrs. Dolan is working on a dress and a couple of alterations and I'd like to have her finish before I go."

"I'm sure you've thought this over carefully," Jamie said, "and if that is what you want, then that is what you should do. We'll miss you here — you know that, of course."

It was not a sincere remark and Jamie secretly hoped Ruth would recognize the insincerity. For a brief instant she felt a savage urge to lash out at the woman, to scorch her with a withering, contemptuous blast. But nothing would be accomplished, she knew and Ruth was on her way out of the picture anyway, probably permanently.

By noon, Ruth had completed packing a small trunk, two suitcases and a couple of boxes and all had been loaded into the Packard. While Black was starting the engine, the three women stood together for a brief moment on the porch steps. Annie, visibly moved, embraced Ruth warmly. Jamie managed a faint smile and a hesitant handshake.

"Write to us when you get to Little Rock," Jamie called as the car moved out to the road.

Dick Thatcher came to the house a few minutes later. He had been working, he told Jamie, in the arroyo north of the lake but had watched the packing of the car and Ruth's departure.

"I gathered Ruth had made up her mind about leaving," he said, "and thought it best to stay out of the picture until after she had gone. How are things going today between you and the doctor?"

"He stayed holed up in the den all night and had only coffee for breakfast. He's deliberately avoiding any conversation with me although he did say a few words to Ruth and Annie. He's not coming back here tonight. At least that's what he told Ruth and she passed it on to me. But before he left, he did something strange. Come in. I want you to see it."

Jamie led the way to the den and pointed to the hand-lettered sign Black had tacked to the door.

W A R N I N G!
Do not enter! Entrance to this room ONLY BY
PERMISSION of the administrator of the Ballantine estate.
Trespassers will be prosecuted!

Thatcher thought a moment. "If I were you," he said, "I honestly wouldn't know whether to be amused or annoyed. I suppose I would be annoyed. The man has absolutely no right to post such a sign in this house. It does tell us something, though. Dr. Black is inordinately sensitive about the den. It is almost certainly tied to the secret he shared with your grandfather."

"Tell me something," Jamie said as they left the interior of the house and settled themselves into the wicker porch chairs. "Yesterday evening you came from the arroyo just north of the lake carrying a spade and a shovel. This morning you were 'working,' you said, in the same area. Yet you told me the search for pre-Indian culture is a fabrication, that your real mission is something entirely different. Want to tell me why you're still poking around in that area? And for what?"

"All right," he said. "We're partners, aren't we? All the way?"

"As sure as you're alive, partner," Jamie said with a smile.

"What I was looking for this morning," Dick said, "and yesterday afternoon, and in fact all the time since I came here, were three rocks. Flat rocks, about two inches thick and six inches across. They're spaced ten feet apart and together serve as a pointer. They should be on the west bank of the arroyo about two hundred paces up from the edge of the lake."

"And you've found nothing?"

"Not a thing, Jamie. But I've only really started. There's a considerable margin for error in the two hundred paces since the edge of the lake advances and recedes as the level rises and falls. Any given point along the arroyo might be twenty-five yards closer to the lake's edge when the water is high, or that much farther away in a dry summer when the lake level is low. And the term 'pace' is imprecise, too. A tall man will normally have a pace several inches longer than average.''

''So what do you plan to do?''

''Keep on hunting. I've stepped off two hundred paces from the present edge of the lake and laid out a strip of ground fifty yards wide to allow for any margin of error. The rocks were originally buried flush with the surface, probably, but must have been covered by dust and sand storms over the years. I just have to probe and keep on probing until I find one. After that, the next two will be easy.''

''And when you do find all three, they will constitute a pointer, you say. Pointing at — what?''

''Unless I am mistaken, they point at whatever permitted John Ballantine and Morgan Black to live very comfortable lives for at least twenty years without working. Of course, I accept the possibility that the flat 'pointer' rocks are no longer there. They could have been removed by persons unknown years ago.''

''That brings us to the interesting question,'' Jamie said, ''of who put the rocks there originally, and when, and what — specifically — they pointed to. For some reason, I think you know exactly what it is.''

''I believe I do, Jamie, and I'll tell you the whole wild, improbable story. But not today. There are a few things I want to check out first. One of them concerns Dr. Black and I have written a friend in Dallas for that information. When I get his reply, I can probably tie the loose ends together. Bear with me just a little longer.''

''There is something,'' Jamie said. ''It may be significant. Perhaps it is just a coincidence, but you have been hunting for your three flat rocks close to a spot grandfather pointed out to me where he said he found old wagon irons years earlier. They showed signs, he said, of having been in a fire. It was thought Indians had attacked several wagons, killed the people and then burned everything.''

''Can you find the place?''

''I don't know, maybe. Grandfather said no trace remains of the wagon irons or anything else at that spot. Probably they just rusted away. I never looked. We can walk over there right now if you wish. It's not more than half a mile.''

Thatcher rose and held out a hand to Jamie. ''I think we should. There is a possibility — a good one — that all of this ties together.''

They walked silently, hand-in-hand. Occasionally Jamie ventured a quick glance at Dick, her head half turned. How warm and strong and protective his hand was. Surely, she thought, she was feeling the first strong stirring of love for him.

She fell to musing over the vagaries of fate and the possibility of predestination. She recalled a powerful sermon the Reverend Burkett had delivered to his congregation a few years ago, on predestination and the rule of compensation. Although she had been bored at the time, it seemed valid now. An unkind fate had taken her parents but had given her Dick Thatcher in return. Predestination? The rule of compensation? Perhaps.

As they reached the arroyo and headed up the old road that ran beside it, another thought occurred to Jamie.

"Someone else has indicated interest in the vanished wagon irons, Dick. Andrew MacPherson. On the day I first met him at the store we were talking about the ranch, legends of Castle Gap, the Horsehead Crossing of the Pecos. I mentioned casually that grandfather had told me the story of a stage holdup and also of the Indian massacre. He seemed surprised. He was familiar with the stage holdup tale but said he knew nothing whatever about Indians having waylaid a wagon train. Then yesterday afternoon, he inquired about it. Said he was certain the wagon irons were the starting point of what he called the Bien Escondido mystery. What do you suppose his game is anyway?"

"I don't know, Jamie. I think he just senses something big is going on and wants to get into the act."

Suddenly Jamie held up her hand. "This is it. At least as closely as I can recall. Grandfather pointed to a spot to the south of the road here where he found the wagon irons. I remember the place from that odd-shaped mesquite."

They moved over to the area, fifty yards or so from the road, and began searching.

"No use looking for ashes or other evidence of fire," Dick said. "The event, if it happened at all, would have been about fifty years ago and there'd be no trace of ashes now. Iron would be a different story. If your grandfather found burned wagon irons at the spot around 1890, some trace of them should still remain."

Without warning, Jamie dropped to her knees, brushed madly at the ground and with a small cry of triumph produced an iron bolt about four inches long and badly eaten by rust but still recognizable.

"There was only about a quarter-inch of it showing above ground. I thought it was just a funny-colored rock at first," she said excitedly. "Does that mean grandpa was telling me the truth?"

"Maybe, maybe. At least, it tends to support his story. Look — why don't we go back to the house and get a couple of those steel-toothed rakes Annie uses to rearrange the gravel in the yard. We've got at least two hours left in the afternoon, time enough to scratch around quite a lot. There may be other bits and pieces buried only inches deep.''

An hour's intensive raking produced two more pieces. One was a second bolt similar to the first, but shorter. Most significant was a piece of strap iron about six inches long with holes bored at each end. At one end a short bolt and metal washer, badly rusted, were still attached. Between the washer and the surface of the strap iron was a fragment of charred wood.

Dick examined it carefully probing and scratching with his pocket knife. ''I'm surprised it lasted so long,'' he said. ''But the wood was probably oak and the charring action would further preserve it. I don't think we need to dig around any more. We have enough evidence now to support your grandfather's story.

''What I don't understand,'' he continued, ''is why he pointed the place out to you. If it's related to his mutual secret with Black, why was he so casual about it? Especially since somebody, probably your grandfather and Dr. Black, apparently went to considerable trouble to remove all evidence. The pieces we found must have been missed.''

''You don't believe the Indian massacre part of the story?''

''No, Jamie, I don't. I think a wagon, or wagons, or perhaps carts were burned here long ago. The Indians were probably an invention of your grandfather. I think he tossed that part in on the spur of the moment when he realized that he had inadvertently said too much.''

On the way back to the ranch house Jamie made a sudden decision. ''I'd like to go in to town tomorrow morning, Dick. You could drive grandpa's Oldsmobile, couldn't you?''

''I don't see why not. I'd like to go to the postoffice. There could be a reply from my Dallas friend. I put a 'General Delivery' return address on the envelope so I should have no trouble picking it up.''

Late that evening as she was preparing for bed, Jamie realized she had made no entry in her diary since the night of her grandfather's funeral. So much had happened in the four days since then. It would be well to put some of them down before she got hopelessly behind.

She pulled the suitcase from beneath the bed. Her mousetrap had been sprung. The carefully-placed thread lay on the bottom of the suitcase and, worse, the snap on the compartment was unfastened. The diary was still inside.

No question about it. Someone had opened the suitcase, taken out the diary and then replaced it.

It must have been Ruth. Dr. Black had gone in to town early, she recalled. Ruth and Annie had been around all day and either could have gone to Jamie's room. But Annie was not the type. Ruth was.

Apprehensive, a little frightened, Jamie replaced the suitcase. She would write nothing tonight. Maybe never again.

Shaken, she fell into a troubled sleep. But she did not hear, shortly after midnight, the squeak of the fourth step.

CHAPTER 20

"Maybe next week I'll teach you to drive, Jamie," Thatcher said. "Other than cranking the engine, there's nothing very difficult. You're strong and shouldn't have any trouble. Once you get the hang of adjusting the choke, spark and throttle, the rest is easy."

"Unless I should have a flat tire," Jamie replied. "That seems to occur rather frequently."

"I'm afraid it does. But it's something you can handle. I'll show you all you need to know. There's also a little knack about shifting gears smoothly but all that takes is a little practice."

Thatcher started Ballantine's Oldsmobile and drove it to the porch steps where they waited for Annie who was making out a shopping list for Jamie. "Annie wants to be let out at her sister's house, Dick, and then you can drop me at MacPherson's store. While I'm taking care of the shopping you'll have time to check your mail. Then maybe we can get a bite at the Texan dining room."

"Sounds fine to me," Dick said as Annie came down the steps and got in.

"Your grandfather made a good selection," Dick said as they rolled smoothly down the Goodland road. "It handles beautifully and rides like a Pullman car. And the color fascinates me."

"I think it was standard black when he got it, Dick. But grandfather always wanted to be different. Anyway, he had it painted yellow before it ever left the garage where he bought it. That's what he told me."

After leaving Annie at her sister's house, Thatcher drove to the MacPherson store.

"I'll be only a few minutes, Dick. Park across the street when you come back. If I'm done first, I'll wait here under the awning."

With a wave and a smile, she watched Thatcher drive off, then turned and went into the store.

Andrew MacPherson was out so one of his clerks filled Jamie's order. MacPherson, the man said, had gone to the bank.

"He asked me to give you a message, Miss Ballantine, in case you came in while he was gone. You are to contact your attorney, Jim Milliken, right away. Mr. Milliken seemed to think it was urgent, Andrew said."

Thanking the man, Jamie immediately gathered up her shopping bags and went to the door. As she left, the Oldsmobile rounded the corner and came to a stop in the street.

"Can't improve on that for timing," Jamie said as Thatcher helped her into the car. "Did you hear from your Dallas friend?"

"Yes, I did, and what he had to say was most interesting. I'd like to have you read the letter. Maybe while we're having dinner."

"There's something we need to do before noon, Dick. Attorney Milliken wants to see me without delay. Something important apparently. Will you go with me?"

"Certainly, Jamie, if that's what you want."

At Milliken's office, his secretary seated Jamie and Thatcher at the conference table where Milliken joined them.

"Miss Ballantine, something of considerable importance has come up. You will recall telling me that your grandfather had apparently consulted his Fort Worth attorneys a day or two before his death about revising the terms of his ranch leases. The thought had occurred to you that he could have done something about a will at the same time. I told you I would contact them. In yesterday's mail I received their reply. Your grandfather did have them prepare a will and he signed it in the presence of two witnesses. They were certain he had it in his possession when he left their offices and it was his intention to file it with the probate judge when he got back to Goodland.

"I explained in my letter that no will had been found in Mr. Ballantine's effects, either his clothing or his luggage, and they found this most disturbing. They sent me a copy of the will, unsigned and unwitnessed, of course."

"Would such a copy have any validity in court, Mr. Milliken?"

"That would depend on the circumstances and the decision of Judge Oliver. There is an outside chance that he might permit probate of a copy of a will even unsigned if it were supported by adequate testimony as could be given by the attorneys who prepared it and saw him sign the original. Such a thing has been done.

"Judge Oliver would have to feel firmly that the original will had been accidentally lost or inadvertently destroyed through no intent of Mr. Ballantine and that at the time of his death, your grandfather's desires as to the disposition of his property were unchanged from when he actually signed the will. Even then, he might refuse to admit an unsigned copy for probate. The decision is his. I spoke to him yesterday afternoon and he said he wanted to think about it for a couple of days."

"And if he decides he can admit the copy. How do we proceed?"

"We would have to file an amended petition, replacing the original petition, asking that the copy be admitted and declared to be the true last will and testament of John Bowie Ballantine. The hearing would have to be rescheduled and on the day of the hearing any persons who might object could be heard."

"May I see the copy you received from Fort Worth?" Jamie asked.

"Yes, of course. It was short and precise. It asked that Dr. Morgan Black be named as executor and devised the sum of $5,000 in cash to Ruth Hazelton and $500 to Annie Murphy. All the remainder of his estate, real and personal, was given to you after payment of any bills and the expenses of administration.

"There is," Milliken continued after a brief pause, "one thing I should mention that has bothered me considerably. That is, who had possession of your grandfather's luggage after it was taken from the train. That person, if the opportunity presented itself, could have removed the will and destroyed it. Assuming, of course, Mr. Ballantine had not already changed his mind and destroyed it himself."

"Ruth Hazelton, Mr. Milliken," Jamie said. "Ruth had it beside her on the rear seat of the car and she took it directly to her room when we got to the ranch."

"I can confirm at least a part of that, Mr. Milliken," Dick said. "She had the suitcase beside her in the car and I saw her carry it upstairs when we got back to the ranch house."

"Dr. Black has said substantially the same thing, Miss Jamie," Milliken said. "I talked to him earlier this morning. Ruth Hazelton was apparently the only one with the opportunity to destroy the original will if it were in the luggage.

"The point, though, is that she had absolutely no reason to do so. In fact, if she destroyed the will she was eliminating your grandfather's bequest of $5,000 to her. If the court found that Mr. Ballantine died without leaving a will, she would have received exactly nothing."

Jamie sat quietly for a moment.

"I guess what you want to know from me, Mr. Milliken," she said, "is whether or not I would be agreeable to a new petition, asking that the unsigned copy be admitted to probate, assuming that Judge Oliver decides he can accept that procedure.''

"That's about it, Miss Ballantine. You understand that your situation under the will, if it is admitted to probate, would be about the same as it is now except for the two specific cash bequests.''

"I understand, Mr. Milliken. I believe, however, that I want to give the matter some thought. It has come at me suddenly and I want to be sure. If Judge Oliver feels he needs two or three days to think, then so do I. At the moment, I am not prepared to give you a definite answer.''

"As you wish, Miss Jamie. The middle of next week will be fine.''

Back in the car, Jamie said nothing while they drove to the Texan hotel. As they parked across from the entrance, she put her hand on Thatcher's shoulder. "I'm not quite ready to go in, Dick," she said. "I have to say what's on my mind first.''

"Could I have two guesses?" Thatcher asked. "One is probably enough.''

"And you'd be right," Jamie said. "I don't want to make an unkind remark, but it will be a very cold day in, well, you know where, before that woman gets a thin dime of Ballantine money. I still get chills when I think of what she tried to do. Bien Escondido is a pretty good-sized spread — seventeen thousand acres, to say nothing of the house and buildings and grandfather's personal property. Considering what it is probably worth, I shouldn't begrudge a bequest of $5,000.

"But to Ruth, I do. $5,000? I'd fight her for $5!''

"Bravo!" Dick cried. "I think you've already made up your mind.''

"Yes, I have. But I want to stall Milliken and Dr. Black too, for a couple of days. Where do you think things will go from here?''

"I'm not an attorney, Jamie, and probably shouldn't comment. But I would guess Mr. Milliken will feel bound as a matter of professional ethics to inform Mrs. Hazelton of the existence of the unsigned will. He may have already done so.

"As soon as Ruth knows the copy might be accepted by the court and finds that you do not intend to do anything about it, she will probably get an attorney and show up at the hearing, asking that the copy be probated. It would be worth $5,000 to her if she gets the job done.

"You would then have to fight probate of the unsigned copy and if you lost, you would have to swallow your anger and accept it or appeal to a higher court.''

"We'll cross that bridge when we come to it, Dick," Jamie said. "Right now I'm cooled down enough to have whatever the noon special is.''

The noon special was chicken and dumplings with a salad of fresh spring vegetables, all highly recommended by the waitress.

After they had ordered, Jamie glanced casually around the dining room. Ruth Hazelton was not there. Since it was now about 12:30, she had probably been in earlier, at least Jamie hoped so. A meeting with Ruth was something she wanted to avoid.

"You said you wanted to show me the letter from your Dallas friend, Dick," she said, changing the course of her thoughts.

"Yes, I do," Dick replied. He removed the letter and handed it to Jamie. It was in a firm, clear script.

> Dear Dick:
>
> I hasten to get this to you since your letter seemed to convey a sense of urgency.
>
> It was not necessary to make an exhaustive search to find answers to your questions. In fact, I hit pay dirt right away. I knew one of my acquaintances had moved here from Denton and a few years ago brought his father (now elderly) to make his home here. I was able to talk to the father, a Mr. Hanson, yesterday evening.
>
> Hanson lived in Denton at the time of the Civil War and up until he came to Dallas, which I think was about 1906. He was well acquainted with Dr. Morgan Black and also with Morgan's father, Dr. Harvey Black.
>
> He says that Harvey Black came to Denton in 1865 and opened an office and his son Morgan joined him several years later. Hanson thinks it might have been about 1870. The father died sometime in the eighties, Hanson said, and Morgan Black left Denton a few years later. Hanson does not know where he went or where he is now, if alive.
>
> I hope this information is what you were seeking. As of now, you are in my debt to the extent of one after-dinner cognac (my choice of brand) and one decent cigar, a fifteen-center at least. I will expect to collect next time I see you.
>
> Sincerely,
>
> George K.

Jamie read the letter a second time before looking up. "Obviously this is our very own Dr. Black who appears to have moved here from Denton which I think is close to Dallas where he and his father Harvey lived shortly after the war. But I don't understand the significance."

"You will, Jamie. Harvey Black moved to Denton in 1865 and his son Morgan joined him about 1870. In 1867, when the events I am going to tell you about occurred, a lawyer named James O'Connor also lived in Denton and was a close friend of Harvey Black. James O'Connor was my maternal grandfather.''

Jamie's eyes widened. "Go on. I think I see a little light.''

"You'll see a lot more in a morment,'' Dick said. He lowered his voice to a near-whisper. "My grandfather O'Connor and Harvey Black, Morgan's father, came into possession in 1867 of a map to treasure of enormous value together with the supporting facts. They were at that time the only living persons with this knowledge.''

Jamie suddenly held up a warning hand her eyes signalling caution. Ruth Hazelton had come into the dining room and had taken a table near the east windows.

"I'll finish the story tomorrow, Jamie,'' Dick said without glancing toward Ruth. "We'll get away from the house so no one can overhear. It's a long story and you'll see the pieces of the Bien Escondido puzzle begin to fit together. All except the last one.''

Finishing their dinner quickly, they left the dining room giving a smile and a nod of recognition to Ruth.

"I'm glad we didn't stop to visit with her,'' Jamie said as they reached the street. "I couldn't have done it.''

Late that evening they sat together on the east porch watching as the near-full moon rose from behind Castle mountain, its silvery reflection marching across the lake to greet them.

"I don't know if I should tell you this or not,'' Dick said, "but it seems to be a time for confessions, at least on my part.''

"Oh, you're forgiven for keeping quiet about your grandfather O'Connor and the Black family,'' Jamie laughed. "Is there more?''

"Yes, indeed. And it didn't happen in 1867, forty-five years ago, but just last night.''

"Last night?''

"It was after midnight. I couldn't sleep. It took me quite a while to figure out why, but I finally did. I couldn't sleep because I wanted desperately to be near you, to hold you in my arms. Please forgive me, Jamie. I wanted you so much that I got dressed, left the foreman's room and came over here to the house. I actually came in and started up the stairs. You really ought to lock the doors.''

"But you didn't come to my room, Dick. Why not?''

"I had taken only three or four steps up the stairs when one of the treads squeaked under my foot. It seemed at once a warning and an accusation. I turned and went back to my room.''

Jamie was silent for a moment.

"What do you think would have happened,'' she said, "if you had come to my door and knocked?''

"I don't know, Jamie. I don't. You would have had every right to have been angry."

"Why don't you come here and find out?" she said in a low voice.

As Dick rose from his chair and moved quickly toward her, she met him eagerly, fiercely. His kiss was warm, gentle and lingering. It reminded her of the delicious smoothness of hot cocoa on a snowy winter night of sledding beside a bonfire at the foot of Gorton's hill.

The heat she felt pulsing through her body came, she knew, not from any bonfire, but from the magic of Dick Thatcher's lips.

CHAPTER 21

"More coffee?" Jamie asked.

They were seated at the kitchen table, breakfast finished. Through the kitchen window Jamie could see Annie in the garden. She would probably be there, Jamie knew, at least an hour. In addition to picking whatever was ready, she would turn irrigation water from the west well into the gardens and do some hoeing.

"I think now would be the right time to continue with your grandfather's treasure legend, Dick. Annie won't be back in the house until at least 10 o'clock."

"All right. Where to start? Maybe a brief review of history would be helpful. Back in 1863, at the height of our own Civil War, Napoleon III of France decided it would be politically expedient to extend French influence in North America, more particularly in Mexico which for several years had been torn by civil war. A French army of more than 30,000 men landed at Vera Cruz, moved inland and occupied Mexico City in June of 1863.

"The Juarez government fled the city and a provisional government was set up. Backed by authority of French guns, the provisional government declared a monarchy and offered the crown, at Napoleon's suggestion, to archduke Maximilian of Austria, brother of Emperor Francis Joseph. Maximilian's rule was violent from the beginning. The dissidents under Juarez waged both conventional and guerrilla warfare with considerable success. In addition, by 1864 it was apparent that the

Confederacy was losing the war between the States. The ultimate survival of Maximilian's empire depended upon defeat of the Union.

"With the victory of the North in 1865, the government in Washington was for the first time able to turn its attention to the gross violation of the Monroe Doctrine which had occurred in Mexico.

"In 1865, an ultimatum was sent by Secretary of State Seward demanding that French troops be removed from Mexico. Napoleon readily agreed. The situation in Europe with respect to Prussia was deteriorating and French taxpayers were loudly protesting the cost of the Mexican venture. The French forces withdrew early in 1867.

"Within a few weeks after the departure of the French, Maximilian's troops, few in number, were defeated and he was forced to flee for his life. He was captured in May 1867 and executed the following month. He had previously sent Empress Carlota to Europe."

Thatcher paused a moment. "Well, so much for historical background. I hope the recitation didn't bore you, but it is necessary."

"Oh, I'm not bored, Dick. Fascinated, rather. Let's see — wasn't the Empress Carlota insane?"

"She became so, Jamie — hopelessly. She's still living, I believe, somewhere in Europe. Now, let me get on with the story.

"In 1867 this part of Texas was a desolate land indeed. Settlements were few, small and primitive, and the space in between them contained more than its share of desperate men.

"A considerable number of these men were Confederate veterans who, after a year of living under carpetbaggers from the North, gave up in disgust and headed for the Rio Grande, thinking to seek their fortunes amid the disorder south of the river. After all, they were soldiers, hardened in the crucible of the combat they had survived. Perhaps they thought their military skills could be peddled to their advantage.

"One group of six, all Missourians, came to Texas in the spring of 1867. They made their way down the Chihuahua trail coming through here and crossing the Pecos at Horsehead and continuing on to Presidio del Norte on the Rio Grande. As they were preparing to cross the river, they met a caravan headed north. It consisted of seven or eight wagons, escorted by a group of fifteen men and one girl.

"The leader was an Austrian who spoke both Spanish and fluent English, a man of distinguished appearance. The girl was his daughter. He was most anxious to obtain information about the route to San Antonio. When informed that there was constant danger of Indian attack, to say nothing of the threat of lawless men of every kind, he promptly made a proposal to the Missourians: Would they agree to turn back to the northeast, he asked, and escort his wagons to a point where they would be reasonably safe from attack. His cargo was valuable, the Austrian said, and he would pay good wages for the service.

"The Missourians conferred quickly and agreed to take the job. After all, they were planning to put their military experience to some good use for pay anyway. It didn't matter whether they did it north or south of the river.

"The first night on the trail, the Missourians made an interesting discovery. The wagons were tightly covered, the canvas lashed down securely. At least one man, and sometimes two, slept by each wagon and the Missourians were told explicitly to stay away from the wagons. In fact, they were asked to make their night camp by the horse picketline, a slight distance from the main group.

"This immediately aroused the curiosity of the ex-Confederates. One of their number was chosen to take a quiet look, if an opportunity presented itself. The chance came on the third night and the man reported back, overcome by excitement.

"He had been able to get into only two of the wagons but found the same in each. First there was a layer of miscellaneous clothing and other items. Underneath these concealing objects, however, there were several boxes and bags and they all contained gold coins. He brought back two or three as proof.

"A council-of-war was held immediately. It seemed likely that what had been found was only a small part of the total cargo and that they were standing within yards of a great fortune.

"They swiftly decided to kill the Austrians and Mexicans and seize the cargo. As I said, these were desperate men. The dark deed was done two nights later, a few miles after they had crossed the Pecos at Horsehead Crossing as the caravan lay in camp near a small lake."

Jamie inhaled quickly. "Our lake!" she said. "That's our lake you're talking about, isn't it, Dick?"

"Yes, Jamie, it is. Let me go on.

"The Missourians attacked quickly and in silence as the men at the wagons lay sleeping. Not even the girl was spared. They lost no time in opening the wagons and found thousands of gold and silver coins, solid gold and silver tableware, candlesticks and vessels of one kind or another, along with chests holding several hundred rings, bracelets and necklaces of diamonds and other precious stones.

"The leader's saddlebags contained documents indicating that he was instructed by the Emperor Maximilian to take this treasure from Mexico across Texas to San Antonio and then to Galveston where arrangements had been made for passage to Europe and eventually to Austria. There it was to be delivered to Carlota. The writings were in

German but one of the Missourians who had been an instructor in a small college before the war was able to translate them sufficiently.

"The six Missourians were now faced with an unexpected problem — what to do with a treasure of such weight and magnitude. It would not be wise, they concluded, to proceed east with it since they would be unable to satisfactorily explain such huge and unusual wealth.

"Not knowing what else to do, they buried the bulk of the treasure after first taking as much in gold coin as they could comfortably carry. They would return later and recover the remainder.

"It was decided to make no tell-tale maps but to put the treasure underground with simple directions they could all remember. They stepped off two hundred paces up the arroyo from the northeast corner of the lake. There, on the west bank of the arroyo, they buried three flat stones, ten feet apart just under the surface. The stones formed the pointer I have been hunting for.

"Following the line made by the pointer, they then stepped off three hundred paces and the treasure was put underground.

"All this took most of the night. Shortly after dawn, they pulled the wagons together and set them afire along with all the other objects. The bodies were tossed into the blaze and the horses turned loose."

"That would have been," Jamie said, "the spot where we found the rusted bolts and the bit of charred wood. Grandfather knew about it from the beginning, didn't he?"

"Yes, he did. And Dr. Morgan Black. And your friend from the general store, Andrew MacPherson, was guessing correctly when he told you the burned wagon irons inadvertently mentioned by Mr. Ballantine were the key to the strange story of Bien Escondido."

Jamie glanced toward the gardens. Annie was still working with her hoe. "Go on with the story, Dick."

"All right. We're approaching the end, now.

"The Missourians left as quickly as possible before anyone could come up or down the trail. Once they got a day's ride to the east, they reasoned, the smouldering ashes near the little lake would not be connected to them. Such incidents were frequent and generally attributed to Indian attacks. The constant wind and blowing dust would soon erase any evidence of the treasure site.

"As the six proceeded eastward from Castle Gap across an empty wasteland, one of them became ill. His condition worsened and when they reached the Concho river he felt unable to continue. After making plans to rendezvous in San Antonio, the other five continued on leaving their companion behind.

"Two or three days later the sick man felt sufficiently recovered to ride again and resumed the journey, only to come suddenly upon the bodies of his five companions a short distance from the trail attended only by buzzards. They had been attacked, apparently by Indians, after having come some forty miles beyond the Concho.

"The man now realized he was the sole owner of an immense fortune. The thought frightened him and he determined to get completely out of Texas as quickly as possible. He would return to Missouri, he decided, and confide in the James boys, one of whom he had met. There was more than enough loot to satisfy everyone. Frank and Jesse would know what to do.

"Just outside the town of Denton, a few days later, he was arrested and charged with being an associate of a gang of horse thieves. While awaiting a hearing on the matter, he requested and obtained the services of a Denton lawyer. That lawyer was my grandfather O'Connor. Before any proceedings could be had, however, his illness returned more severely than before. A doctor was called to attend him and, as you have probably guessed, the doctor's name was Harvey Black.

"The Missourian's condition became worse and it was soon evident that he was near death. When informed of this, the man took Dr. Black and grandfather O'Connor into his confidence. He had, he said, no property except his personal effects, his horse, some gold coin and a tale of hidden wealth. He asked that a good home be found for the horse and that the coins be used to provide a decent burial.

"As for the tale of treasure, he told it in detail to Mr. O'Connor and Dr. Black. They had treated him with kindness and consideration in his dying moments, he said, and it was the only way he could repay. He began to talk and grandfather O'Connor took notes. Two hours later, the sick man lapsed into unconsciousness and died that night.

"The following day grandfather O'Connor pulled the scattered notes into narrative form, beginning at the Rio Grande and ending in a jail cell in Denton. He made two copies, giving one to Dr. Black and keeping the other. He also prepared a rough map as best he could from what he had heard."

"So at that point," Jamie said, "your grandfather and Dr. Harvey Black jointly knew the story of Maximilan's fortune. What did they do about it?"

"Nothing until the following year. There was so much Indian activity and general violence that they felt it would be a foolish risk. In 1868, however, things were quieter and they were able to devote a month to the necessary travel and search.

"They went through Castle Gap and came to the lake described by the dying Missourian. They found the charred remains of the burned wagons. They stepped off the required two hundred paces up the arroyo but could find no trace of the pointer stones.

"They searched for two days with no success. It had been a very dry year and the lake shore had receded considerably causing them to look in the wrong place. On the third day a savage sand and dust storm descended making it impossible to do anything. Discouraged, they gave up and went back to Denton. It was their only attempt to locate the treasure."

"Just one thing," Jamie said. "How and when did all of this information come to you?"

"About three years ago, Jamie. On my twenty-first birthday. My mother gave me a large sealed envelope. She didn't know what was in it, she said. On the outside grandfather O'Connor had written, 'To be delivered to my grandson Dick on his 21st birthday.' Mother said grandfather had given it to her somewhere around 1895, two or three years before he died. I was in the second grade at the time, she recalled.

"The envelope contained the original narrative from 1867 and the map plus grandfather's account of their 1868 expedition. He had added that he believed Dr. Harvey Black had made no further search either and that Black had died in 1882."

"I can see the connection with our Dr. Morgan Black," Jamie said, "but how did my grandfather get involved?"

"I don't know, Jamie. I can only guess that Harvey Black told the story to his son Morgan who later for some reason took your grandfather, his 'best friend,' into his confidence. Anyway, Morgan and your grandfather Ballantine were in it together, apparently as partners."

"Let's see, now," Jamie said. "All the evidence seems to support the premise that grandfather Ballantine and Morgan Black, using the same information your grandfather O'Connor gave you, came here somewhere around 1890 and were able to locate Maximilian's gold and poor Carlota's tableware and jewelry.

"We must also assume that quite a bit of it remains hidden. Black intends to take whatever is left for himself cutting me out completely. He has tried to shoo everyone away from the ranch except himself. That would give him ample time to clean out what remained.

"As for the pointer rocks, it's my guess that they were there just as the dying man said, but were removed long ago. By Dr. Black and my grandfather."

Jamie looked quickly toward the window where a flash of motion caught her eye. Annie was leaving the garden.

"Annie's coming," Jamie said. "Quickly, what do we do next?"

"Let me have three or four more days to probe for the markers. If I find them, I know where they will point — to your grandfather's den. I think this house was built, deliberately, directly over the treasure site. Dr. Black's strange actions make that almost a certainty."

"And if you don't find the stones?"

"Then I think we should force the lock on the den."

"So be it," she said.

CHAPTER 22

"Would you sit here at my desk, Ruth," Morgan Black said as he eased himself into the chair across from her. "I'm surprised, frankly, that you asked for this appointment. As you know, I don't have an office nurse and see patients only occasionally, mostly as an accommodation to the other doctors when they get overloaded.

"Let's see," he continued. "You left the ranch several days ago and as far as I know you were in good health then. Don't you feel well?"

"I feel very well indeed. I don't need professional assistance."

"I should have guessed as much," Black replied. "What can I do for you?"

"It's what we can do for each other, Dr. Black. An even exchange, I think you will agree."

"Go on," Black said.

"I have retained an attorney — Victor Adamson — and he will soon intervene in the Ballantine estate proceedings. He will petition the court to have me declared John Ballantine's common-law wife and, as such, to share the inheritance with Jamie Ballantine."

"I'm not greatly surprised," Black said. "Were you?"

"Was I what?"

"His common-law wife. Did you share his bed? Were you sexually intimate with him, to the point of consummation?"

"Yes, I was. But I am not sure my testimony will be enough. A copy of a will has turned up. As you know, we could not locate an original will, but Mr. Ballantine apparently made one while he was in Fort Worth. He must have changed his mind and destroyed it before boarding the train to come home. The Fort Worth attorneys sent a copy to attorney Milliken and he discussed it with me."

"I have seen the copy and read its provisions," Black said. "I don't know if Miss Ballantine will amend her petition and ask that the copy be accepted as a valid will or not. And I do not know if the judge will permit the probate of an unsigned and unwitnessed copy."

"The point is, doctor, that the will left me a pittance of $5,000. As John Ballantine's widow I should receive half of Bien Escondido. Also, the will contained a specific statement that would cast doubt on any claim of common-law wife status. That statement was a lie, Dr. Black, but I need help in proving it. That's why I have come to you."

"What do you want me to do?"

"I want you to tell the court that you have seen or heard me go to John Ballantine's room at night and return from there early in the morning. Not once, but many times. I want you to say that you have heard the sound of love-making coming from his room."

"Mrs. Hazelton, you are asking me to commit perjury. True, I have often suspected you and John were intimate, but I never really knew. I cannot honestly remember any incidents of that kind."

"Then, doctor, I would suggest that you jog your memory a bit. Work on it. I'm sure that if you do, the facts will come crowding forward in your mind. It would be extremely valuable to you."

"I don't understand, Ruth. How could it be valuable to me?"

"Because if I can't establish my claim, Jamie will inherit everything. Your testimony would be unimpeachable. I am sure I would win. Without your help, Jamie will get Bien Escondido. And everything that goes with it. Particularly the latter which is what interests you the most."

"I don't understnd."

"Yes you do, doctor. You understand completely. There is great wealth hidden out there, worth far more than those cactus-infested acres. I have suspected this for several years and now I'm certain. I don't know where it came from, just that it is there. Until recently you had a partner who shared that wealth. John Ballantine. He's gone now, and you are about to acquire a replacement. Ruth Hazelton."

"All right. Assuming you are correct and, because of my convincing testimony, the court finds that you are John Ballantine's widow and you and Jamie then jointly inherit Bien Escondido. What then?"

"Jamie will leave Bien Escondido. It shouldn't be difficult. She doesn't like the place or the climate. There is no social life whatsoever for a young girl. No men to come calling. There is young Mr. Thatcher and I am sure she is fond of him. He will be leaving at the end of the summer. Who knows? Perhaps she will leave with him.

"I will offer to remain at the ranch and look after things as joint owner. She will probably want to sell her half to me or to someone else.

"After Jamie has left the ranch, I will send Annie on vacation. At that point, doctor, it will be your turn. You will bring into the light what you and John have hidden away and we will divide it."

"Divide?"

"Yes, Morgan, divide. Half to you and half to me. The widow Ballantine."

Morgan Black opened a desk drawer, removed a Havana cigar, bit off the end and lighted it. "Please permit this small luxury, Mrs. Hazelton," he said. "It helps me think and right now I need that very much.

"You have painted a plausible picture but I cannot go along with it. We are talking — and I have told this to no one until now — about the personal fortune of the Emperor Maximilian of Mexico for which people have searched from the Rio Grande to San Antonio since 1867. What is left, after John and I drew upon it for more than twenty years, is probably worth several hundred thousand dollars. Since John's death, I am the only one who knows where it is. It is mine by right of discovery and I intend to keep it. All of it."

Ruth's eyes widened. "What about John's share?" she said.

"He had no share, Ruth. I had the original map and the accompanying directions given to my father in 1867 by the sole survivor of the six men who seized the treasure.

"My father made an unsuccessful search the following year. It was his only attempt and he died in 1882 without trying again. He left the map and directions and an account of what had happened with me before his death.

"For various reasons I was not able to do anything about it for six years. Then, in 1888, I found I was able to get away for a month or so and decided to check out the treasure legend. I didn't want to go alone so I enlisted John Ballantine as a companion. I had known him for several years and liked the man.

"We had no agreement, formal or otherwise, about any partnership. I'm sure we both regarded our trip as an adventure, a vacation somewhat different and more exciting than the usual summer outing.

"Without going into details, we followed the directions and map and located the treasure.

"We were now confronted with the same problem that had faced the men in 1867 — what to do with it. It was Ballantine's idea that we should take out gold coin and some of the more valuable rings and necklaces — items we could carry easily — and then conceal the rest.

"After converting these items into cash one of us should arrange to buy several thousand acres or so encompassing the treasure. We would then have a house built along with the usual ranch buildings, lease some additional land and go into the cattle business.

"It was decided to put the ranch in John's name and let him look after that part of it. Since I was a physician I would move to Goodland and set up a practice there. Together we would be able to keep watch over Maximilian's fortune, extracting what we needed from time to time, in complete safety. My part was to make periodic trips to San Antonio where I would arrange to quietly convert the jewelry and gold into United States dollars.

"And now," Black continued, "that phase is finished. The next and final phase is that I intend to recover all of the remaining items. I am rightfully entitled to them. Miss Jamie has no rights since her grandfather had none. When he got the ranch land, he got his full share of the venture. I provided operating and living funds for John from what we extracted from time to time but that was all. We considered it a proper expense of maintaining the deception.

"And you, Ruth, are entitled to exactly nothing. And if you think I am going to cooperate with you by lying on the witness stand, think again. I know you, Ruth. If your vicious scheme worked and you became a part owner of Bien Escondido, I would never be permitted to set foot on the place again."

For a long moment their eyes locked in an icy embrace.

"You are probably right. After all, who needs you on Bien Escondido? I know, now, all I need to know. It was very crafty to build the ranch house on top of the treasure. To be precise, access to the treasure is through the floor of John's den, isn't it?"

Ruth rose to her feet but made no move toward the door.

"I am going to see Mr. Adamson after I leave here," she said. "I will instruct him to proceed with my petition to be declared John's common-law wife. We will have to get along without your testimony. If I win and become a joint owner of Bien Escondido — well, you are quite right. You will never set foot on the place again.

"If I should lose, Jamie will inherit everything and in that case, I will tell her all I know in return for a third or fourth of what turns up. Maybe she won't give me anything at all. I don't know. But I do know that you, doctor, are all done. I'll see you in hell before you get a nickel more of what's buried under John's den!"

Her face a mask of fury, Ruth turned toward the door. She was still six feet from it when her consciousness dissolved in a blinding flash of exploding colored lights followed by darkness.

Morgan Black stood over her for a moment holding the heavy brass cigar ashtray with which he had struck her just above the left temple. Then he replaced the ashtray on his desk and knelt beside her. With the thumb and middle finger of his right hand, he quickly sought and found the carotid artery. He began to apply pressure cautiously at first, first, then gradually increasing it to completely shut off the flow of blood to the brain but without leaving bruises on the skin.

Beneath his thumb and finger he could feel the surge of heartbeats as the blood struggled to reach the brain with life-sustaining oxygen.

Suddenly, after what seemed an eternity, the heartbeat fluttered violently and then stopped. He continued to apply the pressure for two or three minutes noting that repsiration had also stopped.

Black got to his feet, breathing heavily. There could be no doubt Ruth Hazelton was dead. He removed a stethoscope from his instrument cabinet, knelt again by the body and listened carefully for a full minute. No heartbeat, no respiration.

As he looked down he spoke in a voice that was no more than a whisper. "Surely you must have known, Ruth. You must have known I could not let you leave this office alive."

He crossed the room, glanced carefully into his outer office, then went quickly to the street door and locked it. Returning to the back office, he sat down heavily in his desk chair. He had acted, he realized, without plan, knowing only that Ruth could not be permitted to live.

After a few minutes he checked once more with the stethoscope. Then, taking the body by both hands, he moved it to a point alongside his desk. It would be necessary to explain the bruise on the temple. Striking the desk in falling would be a logical answer.

He went to his filing cabinet and rummaged around before finding the folder with Ruth's records. He had remembered correctly. Ruth had come to him on four occasions during the last few years. Two of those had been to report severe chest pains, rapid pulse and extreme irregularity in heartbeat. He had made a notation on the first of those examinations: *Probable history of rheumatic fever as a child with accompanying valve damage.* The second had reulted in the comment, *Occasional violent spasmodic irregularity indicated.*

It was enough, he thought.

He went to the telephone in the outer office.

"Miss Bessie," he said when the operator answered. "This is Dr. Black. Would you be so good as to ring the Sanderson Furniture number. I'm afraid I have forgotten it."

"Don," he said when Sanderson answered, "this is Morgan Black. I'm sorry to report that I need your services here in my office. I've just lost a patient, Ruth Hazelton. She collapsed and died suddenly from a coronary occlusion. It happened about fifteen or twenty minutes ago and I've been trying ever since to get her heart started without success. It was instantaneous and irreversible.''

Sanderson replied he would be there in ten or fiteen minutes. Black hung up the telephone, went to the street door and unlocked it and then returned to his desk.

As a final precautionary move, he listened once more with the stethoscope. Nothing.

He sat down heavily in his chair. He had not intended that this happen and why he had been so carried away as to impulsively blurt out everything he and Ballantine had so carefully kept concealed, he could not explain.

No matter, he thought. It was done and could not be undone. He had desecrated the Hippocratic Oath and the mark of Cain was upon him. Although it was a terrible price to pay, he realized it had been necessary to preserve the future which he had planned for the son and grandchildren he had never seen.

Tomorrow, he thought, he would chart a new course.

CHAPTER 23

''I think yesterday's probing for the pointer rocks was the last I'll do in that direction,'' Dick said as Jamie poured a second cup of coffee. ''I'm convinced now that your grandfather and Dr. Black removed them long ago just as they did the burned and rusted wagon irons. If the rocks had been still in place I would have found them by now. I don't think the lake shore could have receded that much in dry years or advanced that much in wet years. They just aren't there.''

''I agree,'' Jamie said. ''So what now? The den?''

''I'll get a few tools. Maybe you should prepare Annie for what's going to happen.''

Ten minutes later Thatcher returned with a wrecking bar, a small sledge and a hammer. Annie had gone upstairs to her room somewhat apprehensive. ''I don't want nothing to do with this, Miss Jamie,'' she had said. ''Dr. Black might make trouble.''

The lock gave way after a few sharp blows of the wrecking bar. They stood a moment on the threshold.

"Nothing seems to have changed since Dr. Black let me look in last week," Jamie said. "I'll check out the desk and you can go through the filing cabinet."

"All right," Thatcher replied. "But I have a feeling we're going to find just what Morgan Black said was in here — ranch business records and probably your grandfather's personal correspondence."

A thirty-minute search proved that assumption correct. The desk contained a number of photographs of scenes around the ranch, branding and roundup pictures and many of Jamie's deceased grandmother Ballantine. An entire drawer was filled with miscellaneous mementos of John and Margaret Ballantine's courtship days — a packet of letters tied up in blue ribbon, faded dance programs, invitations to galas. There was a large cameo on a silver chain and a locket containing an unfamiliar picture, a severe-looking woman, probably Jamie's great-grandmother, she thought. A small hardwood box lined with velvet held a collection of rings, pins and brooches.

A second drawer contained only one item: a Colt six-shot revolver, loaded. Another drawer was nearly filled with ammunition, presumably for the pistol and the rifles and shotguns in the wall rack.

The only thing that offered any clue was a leather-bound record book marked "Journal." In it were records of cattle sales, ranch business expenses, purchases, and many pages listing bank deposits and checks issued. There were also dozens of deposit slips in the Cattleman's Bank and a large collection of cancelled checks. John Ballantine had kept careful records.

"What do you suppose this is?" Jamie asked pointing to the inside cover of the Journal. Near the top of the cover page there appeared in handprinted, heavy black lettering:

NE lg mg 32 46

Thatcher studied it for a long time before replying.

"I don't know. It's probably an abbreviation of something your grandfather didn't want to forget and didn't want anybody else to figure out, either. Maybe something will show up that we can tie to it."

The filing cabinet contained only correspondence, much of it personal letters from old friends in east Texas and elsewhere. One drawer was exclusively business correspondence but all apparently ordinary and routine.

As Dick was glancing through the filing cabinet correspondence, Jamie suddenly cried out. "Look at this! I think I've found something. Here at page 100 of the Journal. It's the only item on the page!"

Thatcher bent to look at Jamie's discovery. It was a set of six numbers: 16-32-84.

"I couldn't begin to guess what those other letters and numbers might be," he said, "but this one's easier. It could be the combination to a safe."

"But where's the safe?" Jamie asked. "Certainly not in this room. Could it be in Morgan Black's home in town?"

"I don't think so, Jamie. And don't be too sure about it's not being here. I bet we're within ten feet of it right now."

Thatcher pointed to the floor. "Under the carpet, Jamie," he said. "Let's see what's under the carpet."

It took only a few minutes to move all the furniture from the room except for the heavy desk and the filing cabinet. Thatcher finally cleared them to one side. The carpet had not been tacked down and Thatcher was able to pull it away from the walls exposing most of the floor. There, under the space where Morgan Black's cot had been was a heavy trapdoor three feet square.

"Keep your fingers crossed," he said as he stepped over to the trapdoor and lifted it. The trapdoor opened to a tiny cellar not more than five feet square and somewhat less in depth. A steel safe sat against one of the walls.

"We'll need more light," Thatcher said. He lighted a kerosene lamp, then entered the cellar taking the lamp with him.

The safe was two feet deep, three feet wide and three feet high. Centered on the door and surrounded by a floral pattern were the words, "Victor Safe and Lock Company." The top of the door bore the lettering in red and gold, "J.B. Ballantine." The walls of the cellar were heavy, eight-inch planking and the floor was cement.

Thatcher pulled himself back out into the den and they both returned to the living room to consider what do to next.

"I'm a little puzzled," Dick said. "As you could see, the safe is not very big and considering the probable thickness of its walls and door, the interior space would be rather small. It could, of course, hold a small fortune in gold coins or a large fortune in precious stones or both. But the story grandfather O'Connor recorded mentions many bulky items such as tableware and candlesticks of solid gold or silver. They couldn't possibly be there."

"Maybe grandfather and Dr. Black disposed of the bigger items first," Jamie said.

"Possibly. First thing to do is get the safe open. We'll see what luck we have with the numbers you found in the Journal.

"Right now," he continued, "I'm speculating on how they could have done all this without arousing suspicion. I'm guessing that they constructed the little cellar themselves after the house was built. They were much younger then and could have done it without any difficulty. Placing the safe in the cellar would have been more of a problem but two men could do it using block and tackle. It would undoubtedly have been brought out to the ranch by wagon from the railroad and possession of a private safe would not have been considered unusual then. Lots of people were wary of banks in those days."

They sat in silence for a few moments. Suddenly their thoughts were interrupted by the sound of an approaching car.

"Morgan Black!" Jamie said, fear furrowing her brow.

"I don't think so, Jamie. Doesn't sound like his car."

They went quickly to the porch as the car pulled up. It was a black Model T Ford. Jim Richardson got out.

"I'm sorry, folks," he said, "but I'm afraid I bring bad news. Ruth Hazelton passed away suddenly yesterday afternoon in Dr. Black's office. She had come to him reporting severe chest pains, he said, and had a fatal heart attack while he was examining her. She apparently died instantly. I was in town on business yesterday and heard the news about 4 o'clock. Sheriff Johnson asked me, being the closest neighbor, to drive out this morning and let you know."

For a moment Jamie was unable to speak. "Oh, poor Ruth! I'm so sorry, Mr. Richardson." She realized immediately that she was actually not sorry at all. But then she was overcome with guilt for harboring such an unworthy emotion.

"Is there anything we can do to help, Jim?" Thatcher asked.

"I think not, Dick. The sheriff checked out her room at the Texan about six last evening and found an address book and a few letters from relatives in Little Rock, Arkansas. He was planning to send several telegrams last night asking what disposition should be made of Ruth's body and her personal effects. I suppose they will want her returned to Little Rock since that was her family home."

"Will you come in and have coffee, Mr. Richardson?" Jamie asked.

"Thanks, Miss Jamie, but no. I have more things to do at my place than I want to think about. If anything develops in town that needs your attention — about Ruth, I mean — I'll let you know."

The Model T came to life with a single spin of the crank and Richardson drove off at the head of a small cloud of dust.

They returned to the living room, their excitement over finding the safe tempered by the sobering news Richardson had brought. She ought to tell Annie, Jamie thought, but decided to wait until later. There was nothing anyone could do and Annie was already upset.

Tragedies always came in threes, Jamie believed, and Ruth's death following closely upon those of her parents and her grandfather Ballantine seemed to offer proof of that.

"I think I'll have a go at the safe, Jamie," Thatcher said. "There's no point in sitting here thinking about Ruth."

Armed with the figures from the Journal and the kerosene lamp, Thatcher descended into the cellar. Jamie looked down from the den.

"If I recall how my dad's safe combination worked," Dick said," you turn the knob several times to the right, stopping on the first 16. Then you turn to the left until the second number, 32, comes up the third time. Then you go to the right until the last number comes up the second time around. Then you turn to the left to zero at which point the safe should be unlocked and the door can be opened. Here goes!"

He spun the dial several times stopping at 16, and continued through the sequence, but at the end there was no sound of the falling bolt and the door remained securely locked. He started over and tried again, more slowly. The door remained locked.

"I may have the procedure wrong, Jamie," he said. "I'm not at all sure whether you stop at the second number the third time around or only the second. I'll try it several different ways."

Ten minutes later Thatcher crawled out and sat on the den floor, his legs dangling over the edge.

"I've tried it about every way I can think of, Jamie. Forward, backward, you name it. The frustration is getting to me."

"Wait a minute, Dick," Jamie said. "By forward do you mean starting to turn the knob in one direction, and by backward turning it in the opposite direction?"

"That's it, Jamie."

"Then why don't you try it really backward, starting with 84 and ending with 16? Grandfather might have scrambled the combination to confuse anybody who might find it. Just like he has confused us."

Thatcher dropped down into the cellar again and ran through the reverse combination — 84-32-16 — with no luck.

"Maybe," he said, "your grandfather reversed the numbers in a different way. What I'm thinking of is 61-23-48. I'll try that." Several tries with those numbers were also fruitless.

"I've got just one more idea, Jamie," Dick said. "And if that doesn't work, I'll have to consider becoming an amateur safecracker. Your grandfather's game with numbers may be a double reverse, which would translate into — let's see — 48-23-61."

He turned the dial slowly, carefully. The dull "clunk" of the bolt as it dropped to free the lock was clearly audible to Jamie who responded with a small cry of triumph.

"Come down, Jamie," Dick said holding out his arms. "We should open the door together."

It opened easily, silently, and the light from the lamp clearly illuminated the interior.

The safe was empty.

CHAPTER 24

"I think there is some sort of pattern here," Dick said.

He was seated at the dining room table which was covered with items from the den — correspondence, deposit slips, cancelled checks, receipts. He had been going over them since breakfast.

"The Journal has what seems to be a fairly complete record of receipts and expenditures begining January 1, 1900. I suppose anything prior to that date was discarded. The duplicate deposit slips at the Cattleman's Bank also go back to 1900. I have been trying to correlate them and have found something interesting."

"They don't quite match, I'm guessing," Jamie said.

"That's right. There are some extra deposit slips that can't be tied into any receipts listed in the Journal. There are as many as eight and as few as five per year. These extra deposit slips are all alike in one respect — they were all apparently made out by Cattleman's Bank personnel and presumably delivered or mailed to your grandfather later. What make it interesting is that each one, without exception, carries the notation 'Cashier's Check, Texas National, San Antonio.'"

"What do you think that means?" Jamie asked.

"It can only mean that a San Antonio bank was sending money to be credited to John Ballantine's account at Cattleman's Bank several times a year. And there is absolutely no evidence to indicate the source of those funds."

"I think we know, don't we Dick?"

"Yes, Jamie. Maximilian's lost treasure. I'm not certain about the mechanics of the procedure but I can make a guess.

"To start at the beginning, I think Dr. Black and your grandfather located the treasure around 1890, bought the original ranch property to include the treasure site and had a house and other buildings constructed. But the house was not built directly over the site. The treasure was never under the den as we supposed. The wagon irons and the pointer rocks were removed. The little cellar and the safe were provided to temporarily hold gold coin and jewelry.

"Dr. Black was admittedly fond of San Antonio. He told me so himself when we were tramping around on one of my fake searches. Black said he went there several times a year. I thought nothing of this at the time because I've always liked the place myself."

"Now, however, I know he went there for a specific purpose — to dispose of gold coins, rings, necklaces and other small but highly valuable items which had been stashed away in the safe. Ballantine's share, after conversion into dollars, was sent back by the San Antonio bank. At least that would explain Black's many trips and your grandfather's extra deposit slips.

"While Dr. Black was handling the financial end, your grandfather maintained the ranch as a cover for the operation at least until he got tired of doing it along about 1905. It's significant that even after he quit operating the ranch, the San Antonio money kept coming several times a year just like clockwork."

"I suppose they chose to dispose of the coins and jewelry in small batches to avoid attracting attention," Jamie ventured.

"I'm sure, Jamie. I think they somehow arranged to open the site at a time when they could work without being observed, perhaps once a year, and remove a considerable amount of coins and jewelry.

"We keep talking about coins and jewelry. What about all those other things. Carlota's solid gold table service, the gold candlesticks?"

"I'm getting to that, Jamie. I would guess that they are still right where they were put underground in 1867. I think Dr. Black was afraid of attracting attention if he tried to dispose of them. Anyway, there apparently was no need. The story originally told by the dying Missourian described thousands of gold coins and several hundred rings, bracelets and necklaces. I think the big items are still there."

"And where do you think 'there' might be?"

"That, Jamie, is the next step. Dr. Black cleaned out whatever might have remained in the safe when he left just before posting his sign on the door. My mind keeps coming back to those unexplanable numbers in the Journal. Here, on the cover page. NE lg mg 32 46. I think they're the key to the original treasure site but I'm no closer to figuring them out now than I was when I first saw them."

"There is one person who does know," Jamie said. "Dr. Black. We may have to trick him into giving us the answer. What I have in mind is revising my petition to the court. Instead of naming Morgan Black as administrator, I will ask to be appointed myself. It may be that Milliken and the Judge will not be too happy with that. If so, I'll ask for someone else. Anybody but Dr. Black."

"I think I see where this is leading us, Jamie," Dick said. "If Black realizes he will never become administrator and knowing how you personally feel, it will be clear to him that access to Bien Escondido will be denied. He then might attempt to open the treasure site and remove as much as he could, secretly, if he thought there were an opportunity."

"And that," Jamie said, "is just what he will have. An opportunity. We will arrange to be gone — Annie too — for a couple of days, and somehow see that Dr. Black learns of those plans. When he takes the bait we will surprise him in the act."

"I think it will work, Jamie," Dick said. "Black seems to be driven by some compelling reason to recover all that remains of the treasure even though he is well-fixed already. I think he'll make a try for it.

"There are a few details that need to be worked out but nothing too difficult, I think."

"All right, we're agreed then," Jamie said. "Let's go in to town. If we leave by 12:30, we can be in Mr. Milliken's office by 2. I have to let him know today what I want to do about the copy of the will."

James Milliken appeared, Jamie thought, just a little distant and unsure of himself as he joined them around the conference table.

"I'm sure you realize," he said, "that Ruth Hazelton's unexpected death has altered the Ballantine estate situation considerably. She was mentioned in the will, you will recall, to the extent of $5,000."

"Yes, I remember," Jamie said. "And I have taken that into consideration in my thinking. I have decided to ignore the copy of the will. When things are finally cleared up, I expect to give Annie $500 from my own funds since it was grandfather's wish that she have that."

"That would be very generous of you, Miss Jamie," Milliken said. "Judge Oliver will be glad to know of your decision since he has decided that he could not accept the copy for probate. He told me yesterday afternoon that he simply could not rule out the possibility that your grandfather might have changed his mind and destroyed the original will himself. That leaves things exactly where they were and we can proceed as originally planned."

"Not quite, Mr. Milliken," Jamie said. "I wish to amend the petition in one respect. I do not wish to ask for the appointment of Morgan Black as administrator."

Milliken sat quietly for a moment staring at Jamie, then went to the window where he stood looking out into the street, his back to them. Then he returned and took his seat at the table.

"May I ask, Miss Jamie, what has brought about this decision?"

"It is a personal matter between myself and Dr. Black, Mr. Milliken. I guess you might say I have lost confidence in him for reasons I prefer not to discuss."

"But it was your grandfather's wish," Milliken said.

"Perhaps it was at the time he wrote that note we found in his lock box. But that could have been written several years ago. Circumstances have changed since then."

"But you are forgetting, Miss Jamie, that he also asked to have Dr. Black appointed in the will he prepared only last month."

"I'm not forgetting that at all, Mr. Milliken. In fact, it seems to me that grandfather may have changed his mind and destroyed the will simply because he realized that I should have been named as exeutor and not Morgan Black. I think he regretted having done that."

Milliken sat thinking for a long moment.

"I gather," he said, "that you now wish to be named as administratrix of the estate in place of Black. Very well. I shall proceed with amending the petition. However, I must caution you that Judge Oliver may not go along with this for the reason that you are only a temporary visitor in Texas. The decision will be his but if it should be unfavorable you will have to select another person to serve."

"I'll be thinking on it, Mr. Milliken. And now, if that takes care of the estate matters for today, I think Mr. Thatcher and I should go over to the funeral parlor for a few minutes out of respect for Ruth."

"I'm sorry, Miss Jamie," Milliken said, "but you're too late. Ruth's body was sent east on the 11:10 train this morning. She will be buried, Sheriff Johnson tells me, in the cemetery of a small church just outside Little Rock."

Jamie was lost in thought for a moment. Then she said, "So fast. It all happened so fast. How is Dr. Black taking it?"

"Not well. Not well at all. He has secluded himself in his house and doesn't want to see anyone. I think he blames himself for not being able to save Ruth. But he shouldn't. When those things hit, massively I mean, there's nothing anyone can do. I've seen it several times."

After leaving the law office, Jamie and Dick drove to the MacPherson store where Jamie asked Dick to wait in the car. "I think I should tell Mr. MacPherson about my decision concerning Morgan Black," she said. "He has tried to be helpful and correctly warned me about Dr. Black, even though his motives may have been rather questionable."

MacPherson received her warmly, ushered her to his private office and closed the door.

"I thought you should know, Mr. MacPherson," Jamie began, "that I have just left Milliken's office. I instructed him to amend the petition for probate, eliminating Morgan Black and substituting me. I don't believe Mr. Milliken was pleased with those instructions but he is going to do it. Dr. Black is now out of the picture and will remain out of it. I have you to thank for alerting me to the danger."

"I'm glad you have taken that action, Miss Jamie. But with respect to personal danger, it is possible that you're not out of the woods yet. Dr. Black is a very determined and vindictive man and he may yet decide to take action to recover what is hidden at Bien Escondido. The more I think about it, the more I feel your personal safety is less secure than ever. In short, you need my help more right now than you did when we first discussed the matter. I asked you then if you would consider allowing me to participate in the recovery project, giving me a small share. I repeat that offer now and, to be specific, I would like to have one-fifth of the reasonable value of whatever we may find."

"Mr. MacPherson," Jamie replied, "when you first made that offer, I told you I would take it under consideration. I have done so. Perhaps I am making a mistake but I do not regard Dr. Black as a serious threat. You have been kind and understanding and I am deeply grateful but I have decided to work this thing out alone."

"You're sure you won't change your mind, Miss Jamie?"

"I don't think so," Jamie replied. "I've thought about it a lot."

"Then I wish you luck," MacPherson said, moving to the door and opening it for Jamie. She murmured her thanks and left the store as quickly as possible wondering if she had handled the matter correctly.

MacPherson watched as the Oldsmobile moved briskly down the street. Thirty minutes later he stood outside the door of Morgan Black's house and rang the bell. There was no immediate response.

After the third ring of the bell, Black opened the door with a frown of annoyance. "I'm not available, MacPherson," he said. "Get one of the other doctors."

"They can't help me, Morgan. Only you can. What I need is ten minutes of your time to discuss a matter of importance and urgency."

Black stepped back and held the door open. "Come on in, then," he said. "I hope it's important. I'm not feeling well as you can see." He led the way to the living room where the two men took chairs facing each other.

"I'll get right to the point, Morgan. Money. Lots of it. What is left of a fortune hidden on Bien Escondido. You and John Ballantine have tapped it for years a little at a time to avoid attracting attention. Now Ballantine is gone and you are the only person who knows where it is. You want to get what's left now, before someone beats you to it.''

"Rubbish. Sheer fantasy. Where did you get such a wild idea?''

"Not wild at all, Doctor. I've been wondering about you and Ballantine for a long time but it was only this spring that some missing pieces fell into place. This part of the country is rich in legends of lost mines, buried treasures. Once in a while one gets found. You and Ballantine were among the few lucky ones.

"And I know about the periodic trips to San Antonio and the remittances back here. And the locked den to which only you and John had access. Between the two of you, it was guarded constantly. Who's there to guard right now, Morgan? Aren't you worried?

"I also know about your scheme to move into the ranch house after being named administrator of the estate and your plan to get everybody else out of there on some pretext or other. Oh, I know, all right. Miss Jamie told me. I have her confidence you see. You do not. And you will be interested to know that today she instructed Jim Milliken to revise the probate petition to remove you as administrator and to have herself named. She told me this less than an hour ago. As I see it, that just about finishes your chances. Except for one.''

Dr. Black, whose face had been expressionless, turned now to look at MacPherson. "Except for one?'' he said.

"Yes, Doctor. Your last chance is, frankly, me. I believe I can help. If I am correct, you are past seventy. Although you are not in poor health, you are certainly not as strong as you once were. Not strong enough to do alone what will be necessary.''

"And what, Andrew, do you reckon will be necessary?''

"A combination of planning, timing and physical work, Morgan. We — and you will note that I am including myself already — will have to recover the remaining items or as much as we can surreptitiously and under cover of darkness. Jamie, Annie and that man Thatcher will have to be elsewhere.

"Perhaps my wife and other ladies can plan a dinner party in honor of Miss Jamie. Thatcher would be invited too. We would arrange for her to stay overnight in town. Annie would be taken to her sister's house and Thatcher to the hotel. That's an initial thought. Possibly some other scheme might be better. Anything to get all three of them away from the ranch all night. We would only have one chance.''

"You will pardon this observation, Andrew,'' Black said, "but I must assume that you are not approaching me with these thoughts out of personal affection. Just what do you want?''

"I'm not a greedy man, Doctor. You're still the principal party. I'm an assistant. I want one-fifth of the cash value of what we can remove."

"Agreed," Black said as the two men shook.

"I'll be in touch as soon as I get something definite worked out," MacPherson said as he left the house.

Morgan Black went directly to the kitchen and took a glass tumbler from a cabinet. Carrying it to the pantry, he selected a bottle and poured an inch of Kentucky whiskey. Then, facing the direction of a distant Nebraska, he raised the drink in salute.

"Wish me luck, son," he said and drained the glass.

CHAPTER 25

The Reverend Jackson had one undeniable virtue. He kept his sermons short and, as a bonus, he refrained from reference to eternal damnation and the fires of hell awaiting unrepentant sinners. All in all, Jamie's idea that they should come to town to attend the morning services and then have Sunday dinner at the Texan dining room was a good one, Dick realized. A refreshing change of pace.

Following the benediction and the usual handshaking at the church door, they drove the several blocks to the Texan, parking the Oldsmobile on the side street.

"I'd like to get in ahead of the crowd, if possible," Dick said, "so we can start back as soon as we can. Even though it's broad daylight and Annie is at the ranch, I'm a little uneasy."

Taking a table by one of the windows, they studied the menu and ordered southern fried chicken, proclaimed to be a specialty of the house. The regular red and white checkered tablecloths had been replaced by white linen for Sunday.

As the waitress disappeared into the kitchen, Jamie, who was facing the hotel lobby, saw Andrew and Emma MacPherson enter the room. She could not avoid an uneasy feeling. Only a couple of days ago she had rejected MacPherson's offer. She glanced away hoping the MacPhersons would not notice them. But it was not to be. She saw them advancing, warm smiles on their faces.

"How nice to see you," Emma MacPherson said as Dick rose from his chair. "Please do be seated, Mr. Thatcher."

"Not only nice but very fortunate," MacPherson said. "Saves me a trip out to your ranch. I was planning to drive out there this very afternoon. Explain, will you Emma?"

"What he means," Emma MacPherson said, "is that he was planning to bring an invitation to a small social affair at our house. I have felt a little guilty that nothing has been done to help you meet people in town who were close friends of your grandfather. I am planning an afternoon tea for several ladies, honoring you, followed by a dinner that evening. We would like to have you, Mr. Thatcher, as our guest also, at the dinner. If it would not be an imposition, we would be pleased to have you say a few words about your scientific studies in the area. People are very interested.

"I'm planning this for Tuesday afternoon and evening if that is agreeable. We would like you to be our guests overnight so you wouldn't have a long drive back to the ranch in darkness. We have two spare bedrooms so there is no problem. I do hope you can accept."

"It's very gracious of you to think of me," Jamie said. "Could Mr. Thatcher and I discuss this during dinner and let you know before we leave?"

"Certainly, Jamie, certainly," Emma replied. "But please say yes. I'll be very disappointed otherwise."

As the MacPhersons moved to a table across the room, Jamie turned to Thatcher. "What do you think?" she said.

"I think we're very lucky. I've been puzzling for two days over how to set the trap for the good doctor and now the MacPhersons have done it for us. All the better, too. The initiative was theirs. If Black should have any suspicions, they will be neatly sidetracked.

"I know now exactly how we should proceed. Accept the invitation for yourself. I will tell Mrs. MacPherson that I am unable to attend since I have made plans to go to Fort Worth on the Tuesday morning train, to return Thursday. However, I will bring you and Annie to town that morning. I'll explain the rest of it after we're in the car. Trust me, Jamie. I know it will work."

"I do trust you, Dick," Jamie said. "Isn't it exciting?" She gave Thatcher an affectionate smile realizing once again how much she had come to depend upon him.

The MacPhersons looked up from their study of the dessert menu as Jamie and Dick came to their table. "I hope you've decided favorably, Jamie," Emma said.

"For myself, yes, Mrs. MacPherson. It's very kind of you to plan this. I think I need to get away from Bien Escondido if only for a short time. So many things have happened."

"And you, Mr. Thatcher?" Emma said.

"I appreciate the invitation," Dick said, "but I'm afraid I won't be available. I've made plans to go to Fort Worth Tuesday morning on the 11:10 train and return Thursday. I can bring Jamie and Annie to town if there is some way for them to get back to the ranch Wednesday."

"Why couldn't Jamie just stay with us an extra day, Emma?" MacPherson suggested. "She and Annie could then go back out to the ranch Thursday afternoon when Mr. Thatcher returns. That place will keep for another day without any help."

Jamie thought a moment. It would be best to let Dick handle this suggestion so it would fit into whatever plan he was making.

"I don't see why not," Dick said. "Jamie would probably enjoy the extra day in town."

"There is one thing, Mr. MacPherson," Jamie said. "I would like to ask you to take a message to Dr. Black. I don't want to speak to him personally but I want him to be informed."

"I'll be glad to help in any way possible, Jamie," MacPherson said.

"I believe I told you," Jamie said, "that Morgan Black would not be permitted to come to Bien Escondido again. I realize, however, that he may have personal things at the ranch which he should be permitted to pick up. It will be agreeable for him to make one trip to reclaim anything he has out there but I insist that this be when I am present.

"I am concerned he might come out while I am in Goodland Tuesday and Wednesday. Mr. Thatcher will be in Fort Worth and Annie will be at her sister's house so no one will be home at the ranch.

"The message I want you to take to Dr. Black is that he can come out on Friday or Saturday to get his things but not earlier. Please be sure to explain why, that there will be no one at the ranch. If you can tell him this today or the first thing Monday, I will greatly appreciate it since I definitely want him warned to stay away before I leave the ranch Tuesday morning."

"I understand your concern," MacPherson said. "I'll make a point to look him up this afternoon and you can be sure that I will give him your message."

As they drove away from the Texan Jamie turned to Thatcher. "All right, Dick," she said. "I can't wait a minute longer. Tell me — how will it help if you go to Fort Worth Tuesday morning?"

"It wouldn't, of course," Dick replied. "But I want them to think I have gone there. To make that crystal clear for Dr. Black I plan to buy a round-trip ticket to Fort Worth and board the train Tuesday morning.

Unless my guess is wrong, he'll be watching. I'll then get off the train at the first stop east of town. The westbound train from Fort Worth comes along a little later and gets to Goodland at 2:15. I'll be on it.

"You see," he continued, "the way things are set up now, you'll be at the MacPherson house Tuesday night and Wednesday night. Annie will be at her sister's house. And I will be in Fort Worth on those two nights. At least, that is what they will believe. Actually, I'll be in hiding at the ranch — a reception committee for the good doctor."

"How will you get out to the ranch?" Jamie asked.

"I plan to put the Oldsmobile in the livery across from the station. I'll get off the last car which is far enough away from the station that the agent won't recognize me even if he's paying attention. Anyway, I'll get over to the livery in less than two minutes and drive back to the ranch. The possibility of Dr. Black seeing any of this is next to zero.

"Congratulations, Jamie" Thatcher continued, "on your quick thinking. By sending that message to Dr. Black through MacPherson you guaranteed he will immediately begin preparations to open up the treasure site Tuesday night. He would have Wednesday night for a second shot if necessary."

They left town immediately and headed for the ranch, stopping only a moment to exchange greetings with Jim Richardson who was inspecting a fence near the road.

"I want to do a little experimenting," Thatcher said as he stopped the car at the porch steps, "and we have the rest of this afternoon and all of Monday for it. Just in case Dr. Black doesn't take the bait."

"I suppose you mean the mysterious letters and numbers."

"Yes. NE lg mg 32 46. No question in my mind that these are directions for the original treasure site. NE probably means northeast. The lg mg somehow comes across as large main gate, which I suppose is the one with the Bien Escondido sign. If that is the starting point, it would be too far from the arroyo. But it won't hurt to give it a try."

The large mantel clock in Dr. Black's living room struck 3 o'clock when Andrew MacPherson rang at the door.

"It's done," MacPherson said. "All taken care of and very smoothly, believe me." He explained the arrangements.

"I was worried Thatcher might decline the dinner invitation and stay out at the ranch but luck was on our side," MacPherson said. "I'd rather have him in Fort Worth than in Goodland. And we have two nights instead of one."

"I believe," Black said after thinking a moment, "I ought to go out there Tuesday night. One night may be enough and that would leave Wednesday in reserve if something should happen. And it would be much better, Andrew, if you did not accompany me. As host, you'll be expected to be at the dinner. You can keep a close eye on Miss Ballantine, discouraging or preventing any return to the ranch earlier than Thursday afternoon.

"Thatcher we won't have to worry about. He'll be in Fort Worth. I plan to make sure he boards the train."

"All right, doctor," MacPherson said. "You take it from here. I'll handle the situation in town and the ranch part is up to you. We can meet right here Wednesday afternoon. And, oh yes, before I forget, the official reason for my calling on you this afternoon is to warn you by Miss Ballantine's specific instructions, to stay away from Bien Escondido until Friday or Saturday at the earliest."

"Tell her," Black said. "You delivered the message and I nodded my head. You don't need to tell her which way."

CHAPTER 26

"Everything's in the car, Jamie," Dick said, "except for whatever Annie is taking along."

He suddenly placed both hands of Jamie's shoulders. "Wish me luck for tonight," he said. "We probably won't have another chance to talk this morning."

"I'll do more than that," Jamie said as she moved into his arms and eagerly accepted his kiss, pressing her body against his. "That's not only for luck but to seal our partnership."

Five minutes later Annie appeared with her suitcase and took her place in the back seat of the Oldsmobile. As they passed through the ranch entrance gate, Thatcher recalled his efforts on the previous day.

He had concentrated his search in an area northeast of the gate and had examined the ground in that general direction as far as two hundred yards. There had been nothing. Actually, it was only something to do while waiting for the main event.

After leaving Annie at her sister's house, Thatcher and Jamie drove to the MacPherson store. MacPherson received them cordially and took Jamie's suitcase.

"I'll drive her out to the house in a few minutes, Mr. Thatcher. Would you care to come along? I could drop you off at the station on my way back here. You can leave John's Oldsmobile parked behind the store if you want."

"Thanks, Mr. MacPherson, but I doubt there's that much time to spare. And for the car, I think I'll leave it in the livery across the street from the station. It'll be handy when I return Thursday."

"Enjoy your brief vacation from the rigors of ranch life, Jamie. If Mrs. MacPherson serves homemade ice cream tonight, don't tell me about it or I'll regret having gone."

As MacPherson and Jamie entered the store she looked back for an instant with a quick smile. Then they were gone.

At the livery, Thatcher obtained permission to park the Oldsmobile near the back of the building. "I don't want it to be in your way," he said. He paid the fifty cents storage charge in advance.

He purchased a round-trip ticket to Fort Worth. The train would be about five minutes late, the agent said. That was fortunate, Thatcher thought. It would allow plenty of time to make the switch to the west-bound train. At 11:05 he left the waiting room and took a position on the platform where he could be plainly seen from all directions. Might as well make it easy, he thought.

Only four other people were boarding and the stop was brief. As he took a seat in the chair car, Dick thought things were going well, almost too well. He went over their plans to see if any flaw existed. He could find nothing.

Ten minutes later he spoke to the conductor and explained his need to leave the train at Indian Wells. He had forgotten to pack some important documents which he would need in Fort Worth. Without them the trip would be useless.

"Give this to the agent when you get back to Goodland," the conductor said, making notations on a small green form and handing it to Thatcher. "This will give you credit for the unused portion of your Goodland-Fort Worth ticket."

Thatcher left the train and purchased a one-way ticket back to Goodland. The west-bound train was not due for nearly an hour so he bought a sandwich and coffee at a small diner a block from the station and spent thirty minutes looking over a couple of dog-eared newspapers lying on the counter. They were from the previous week, he noted, but the first he had seen for ten days. How quickly one could lose touch with the world.

The west-bound express ran twenty minutes late and arrived in Goodland at 2:40. Dick found it was not possible to leave from the last car since it was a Pullman. The car next to it was a comfortable distance from the station, however, and before stepping down, Thatcher noted that the agent was busily loading his baggage truck. He moved quickly across the tracks and into the shelter of the livery barn. No one paid any attention, he was sure.

Explaining casually to the livery owner that there had been a change in his plans, Thatcher cranked the Oldsmobile. As he drove into the street, he had an uneasy feeling that the man was a little doubtful about his sudden reappearance. It was the weakest part of his plan. If Morgan Black should check on the car he would be instantly alerted. Nothing could be done now. The plan either worked or it didn't.

The road was nearly deserted. Thatcher met only two cars and did not recognize either. The Richardson ranch buildings were the only ones close to the road and no one was in sight.

Arriving a few minutes before 5 o'clock, Thatcher took the cutoff to the left and followed the road to Castle Gap. He crossed the arroyo and came to a spot where the road dipped into a shallow depression. He could hide the car here since the top was down. It was less than a hundred yards from where he and Jamie had found the rusted bolts and charred wood.

Thatcher went directly to the bunkhouse, changed into working clothes and went to the main house. He had decided to post himself on the second floor since by going from room to room he could observe from the windows in all directions and still remain concealed.

It would be well, he thought, to select some sort of hiding place just in case Black should come into the house. The large wardrobe in John Ballantine's room would be perfect, he decided. In checking it out he found a pair of binoculars hanging from a hook and realized they could be helpful. There was not going to be much moonlight and the binoculars would provide useful light amplification especially if Black should go any distance away from the house.

There was one more thing he needed and it was in the den. As he came down the stairs, the sunlight suddenly diminished. Shadows which had been sharply distinct began to melt away. Going to the kitchen he looked out the west window and saw a bank of heavy clouds begining to obscure the late-afternoon sun. An unfortunate development, he thought. A heavy rainstorm might cause Black to postpone his trip until Wednesday night. Any delay would increase the chances that the trap would never be sprung.

In Ballantine's den Thatcher thought carefully for a moment and then took down a model 94 Winchester carbine from the gun rack. It was a standard item on any western cattle ranch, a 30/30. It was not loaded but Thatcher found a box of cartridges in a desk drawer and fed five rounds into the magazine and put another five in his pocket. Black would not be armed, he thought, but it would be good to be prepared.

He pulled a chair up to the north window of John Ballantine's room. It offered a clear view of the road from town.

He speculated how Black might plan things. Probably he would arrive about dusk in order to avoid driving at night with undependable acetylene lights. That would give him seven or eight hours to work and he could start back to town at first light tomorrow morning.

It seemed to be getting dark rapidly and Thatcher went to a west window to examine the sky. The cloud mass he had noted earlier had grown and there were now two separate, towering thunderheads rising from a black and ominous base, each wearing a golden crown from the dying sun. Occasional fitful flashes of lightning illuminated them. Returning to the window, Thatcher resumed his watch.

Somewhere around 7:30, as near as he could guess, Black's Packard appeared, came through the ranch gate and stopped beside the shop building. The bait had been taken.

Morgan Black got out of the car, swept the area quickly with his eyes and then removed several things from the Packard. One was a small kerosene lantern and, although it was not yet fully dark, Black lighted it. The other items were several wooden boxes , what appeared to be some grain bags, and a spade and shovel.

As Thatcher watched through the binoculars, fascinated, Black took the lantern and the spade and went immediately to the water tower that served the gardens and the corral. Apparently he was going ahead without regard to the threat from the sky. Probably, Thatcher thought, he planned to do as much as he could and then take shelter in the nearby shop building if the storm broke.

Placing the lantern on the ground beside the leg of the water tower, Black removed a small instrument from his pocket and held it in front of him. He seemed to be sighting along or through it. It could be only one thing, Thatcher thought. A compass.

Suddenly it was all clear. The NE lg meant the northeast leg of the water tower where Black was now standing. The mg 32 had to mean an angle of 32 degrees from magnetic north. With the starting point and the direction determined, the 46 must be the distance to the treasure.

Taking the spade, Black moved off toward the gardens. Thatcher began counting the paces. At the forty-sixth pace Black stopped and sank the spade into the ground. Thatcher sprang from his chair and almost cried out. The bean patch! The treasure was directly beneath the bean patch! How many times had Ruth and Annie planted, tended and harvested there, not knowing how close they were to Maximilian's fortune.

Black turned now and retraced his steps to the water tower. He took another compass reading. As he sighted along his arm, hand and extended finger, a single large raindrop splattered against the bedroom window. The storm was upon them.

Black glanced quickly at the sky and trotted out toward the spade. He pulled it from the ground and drove it in again about three feet to one side. It was his last act.

Momentarily blinded by the intensity of the lightning bolt and shaken by the simultaneous crash of thunder, Thatcher dropped the binoculars and pressed his hands to his eyes. It was a full minute before he was able to see again. Then, his eyes misty and uncertain, he levelled the glasses on the bean patch. Black had disappeared.

A moment later the deluge descended accompanied by large hailstones reducing visibility to zero. The rain continued to fall heavily for ten minutes, and then ceased as suddenly as it had begun.

For the next two hours, Thatcher observed the bean patch and the shop building. No movement whatsoever. The lantern which Black had left at the leg of the water tower was not visible. Probably the intensity of the storm had extinguished it, Thatcher thought.

By 10 o'clock a hesitant half moon broke through the remaining fragments of the storm cloud and visibility improved. Removing the binoculars, Thatcher picked up the rifle and went downstairs and out of the house. Now that Black had given him the answer to the puzzle, he rationalized, there was no point in delaying their confrontation.

He reached the shop building and continued into the garden. Black's body was lying beside the spade. There was no question about it. Dr. Morgan Black was quite dead.

CHAPTER 27

"I'm glad you came, Miss Jamie," Jim Milliken said. "I've been hoping you would ever since I learned about the tragic accident. There are important matters you should have legal counsel on. Mr. Thatcher could be involved also and I'm happy he has accompanied you.

"In the first place, the inquest yesterday determined that Dr. Black died Tuesday night as a direct consequence of having been struck by lightning. Dr. Adams testified that the electrical charge entered the right shoulder, crossed his chest, passed down his left arm and then followed the spade into the ground."

"He probably would be alive today, Mr. Milliken," Thatcher added, "if he had not been driving the spade into the soil. It made an excellent ground and I'm sure attracted the charge."

"Quite possible," Milliken replied. "The important thing, however, is that Black's death has been found to have been accidental. That brings us to what must be considered next."

"That," Jamie said, "is the question of what Morgan Black was doing in the vegetable garden at Bien Escondido, alone and at night, during a violent electrical storm."

"Yes indeed, Miss Jamie," Milliken said. "The question demands an answer. And a second question is almost as intriguing as the first. What was Mr. Thatcher doing? He was also at Bien Escondido hiding on the second floor of the ranch house by his own admission to Sheriff Johnson. And this after an elaborate pretense of having gone to Fort Worth for a couple of days."

For a long moment there was silence. When Thatcher spoke, it was to Jamie. "I think you should give Mr. Milliken the facts, Jamie. He is acting as your counsel and will hold what you say in confidence."

"Yes, I will," Milliken replied. "And I would like to suggest, with all due respect, complete honesty. There has been considerable game-playing up to now and the time for that has passed."

"All right," Jamie said. "Let me first say that I believe a substantial fortune in gold coins, jewelry and other items is buried on Bien Escondido — a lost treasure found years ago by grandfather Ballantine. I'm sure you know this area is rich in legends of such hidden treasure. I came to this conclusion from remarks my grandfather made before he died and from various clues we discovered in grandfather's den. I sought Mr. Thatcher's help. That explains his involvement.

"I believe grandfather had an arrangement with Morgan Black whereby Black performed two services. One was to stay at the ranch and keep watch whenever grandfather was gone. The other was to peddle coins and jewelry in San Antonio. They did this in small batches several times a year. Black probably shared on some sort of percentage basis."

"If this is true and apparently went on for years," Milliken asked, "is it not possible that whatever was there has already been taken out? Why do you feel there is a substantial fortune — your words, I believe

— still hidden?''

''Because ever since grandfather's death, Dr. Black has been trying frantically to get me and everybody else away from the ranch. It was his plan to move out there under the pretense of looking after things as administrator of the estate. Once in possession, with nobody around to interfere, he could have taken everything for himself. He would have told me nothing, I'm sure. When all of his efforts in this direction failed and he learned that I was asking for my own appointment as administrator, I felt he would make some move to take what remained of the treasure surreptitiously. That feeling was correct and it explains what Morgan Black was doing in the vegetable garden last Tuesday night.

''As to Dick Thatcher's activities, I confess that we deliberately spied on Dr. Black that night. We arranged for him to believe there would be no one at the ranch Tuesday or Wednesday nights. We wanted him to show us the treasure site. We knew it was near the ranch house. He did it, Mr. Milliken, and his greed cost him his life.''

Milliken sat in thought for a few moments before speaking.

''I believe, Miss Ballantine, that the time has come for you and Mr. Thatcher to let this matter be handled by the proper authorities. If you have given me the facts correctly, then what we are dealing with is 'treasure trove' which has a distinct treatment under the law. To qualify as treasure trove, the subject property — coins, jewelry, gold bars, whatever — must have been truly lost, not just temporarily hidden, for a substantial period of time with its owner unknown.

''A finder is entitled to retain it if no one appears and establishes ownership to the satisfaction of a court having jurisdiction. There is a time limit for this. I believe it is one year. Under certain circumstances the find would have to be shared with the owner of the land, but in this case your grandfather was both the finder and the owner.''

''You have said that we should let this be handled by the proper authorities, Mr. Milliken,'' Jamie said. ''What should we do?''

''I think Sheriff Johnson should be given the facts you have just given me. He should be requested to arrange for excavation of the treasure site under his direct supervision. Whatever is removed should then be inventoried in your presence and impounded in a safe place until proper disposition can be made by the court.

''I have already revised the Ballantine probate petition to ask for your appointment but I think the petition should be revised again. It should list the items found in the bean patch, as inventoried, and should allege that this property falls under the treasure trove definition and should be found by the court to belong to the John Ballantine estate. Since you are undoubtedly John's only legal heir, it would all be yours when the estate is closed. By including this in the estate proceedings, the matter of notice to the public would be complied with. I would not anticipate any difficulty whatever, just that it will take longer than it would normally."

"Will you make the necessary arrangements, Mr. Milliken?" Jamie asked.

"Tomorrow is Saturday and I'll see Johnson this afternoon. Hopefully he can start in the morning. Don't be surprised if I show up too. This whole thing is fascinating! I can't wait to see what comes to light under the beans."

The services for Morgan Black were scheduled for 2:30 that afternoon at the Presbyterian Church but Thatcher and Jamie headed directly for the ranch.

The story of Black's death had spread across town with astonishing speed, gaining lurid overtones along the way. Some of these, Jamie was sure, would suggest an improper relationship between herself and Dick Thatcher. They had decided the situation was best handled by staying away.

The Presbyterian Church was filled beyond capacity. Fifteen or twenty people, unable to find seats, listened from the entry and steps.

"About fifty-fifty, I would guess," Andrew MacPherson mused as he and Emma left the church. "Half of them were Morgan's close friends or at least more than casual acquaintances. The other half came because of morbid curiosity. It's not every day that one of the town's leading citizens gets struck by lightning at night in a bean patch forty miles from home."

"Is that the end of it, Andrew? For us, I mean?"

"I'm afraid so, Emma. We gave it our best shot and it failed. Jamie Ballantine doesn't need us now. I can only hope no one finds out about our arrangement with Black. I don't think Jamie suspects. After all, we were only complying with her request when we told Morgan there would be no one at the ranch Tuesday night. She was emphatic about our doing this, you remember."

"Maybe," Emma said, "it's for the best. I'm beginning to think there must be some sort of curse on whatever is out there. Three people died in less than a month."

"They say that such deaths come in threes, Emma, so that should be the end of it. I'm sorry about the house, though."

"The house?"

"Yes, Emma. I had the plans drawn in my mind for a new house for us on Travis Avenue. When we got our share."

CHAPTER 28

The excavation work was well underway by 10 o'clock Saturday morning. Sheriff Johnson had brought four workmen whom he had made special deputies and his first act was to rope off an area about twenty feet square with a stake in the center marking the point where Dr. Black's spade had been found. Jamie, Dick Thatcher, Sheriff Johnson and James Milliken stood just inside the rope watching intently.

When the workmen had dug down about two feet, Johnson removed some of the dirt from the bottom of the hole. "Take a look at this," he said. "You can see it's a mixture of two or three different kinds of soil. Proves the spot has been excavated before and then back-filled. This is the place, all right."

The first object was found about 10:30: a silver candelabrum. Directly beneath it were dozens of knives, forks, spoons and ladles, all solid silver except for the blades. To one side of the initial find, a deputy uncovered a small brass chest about ten inches long and five inches wide. There was no lock and upon opening it Johnson discovered a number of rings, bracelets and necklaces. Two of the necklaces were of beautifully matched large pearls, Jamie could see.

The brass box had once been lined with blue velvet now badly deteriorated. Only fragments remained. Jamie was sure it had been Carlota's personal jewel chest. In rapid succession, the diggers now uncovered large numbers of gold and silver coins in several oak boxes, more candelabra and an assortment of platters, bowls and serving plates, all either silver or gold.

At noon Annie came out to the gardens carrying a platter of sandwiches, a large pitcher of lemonade and several glasses. Jamie was too excited to eat.

By 1 o'clock, the excavation was done. The bottom of the original hole had been about six feet, apparently, and there was no point in digging deeper, the sheriff said, since the soil had obviously never been disturbed. The same was true on all sides. On Johnson's instructions, the deputies carried all of the items to the porch for inventory before placing everything in sealed boxes. The boxes would be stored in the vault of the Cattleman's Bank.

There were 2,278 silver coins of various types and sizes but only 355 gold coins.

"I'm guessing," Thatcher said to Jamie as they stood some distance away from the others on the porch, "that your grandfather and Dr. Black concentrated on gold coins, gold bars or ingots if there were any and possibly jewels. They apparently preferred to leave the silver and the large pieces for attention at some future time. Why the brass jewel box was not put in the safe I can't imagine. Probably overlooked."

"Your original assumption was obviously correct," Jamie said. "I mean, that the treasure site was tapped infrequently, once a year perhaps, maybe only every other year."

"I think so, Jamie. And when they opened the hole, they loaded up the safe with high-value gold and jewelry, enough for several San Antonio trips by Black."

The inventory was completed by mid-afternoon. Sheriff Johnson made two copies, one for himself and one for Jamie. He signed each copy and then had Jamie sign them and Mr. Milliken as attorney for the Ballantine estate. Dick Thatcher also signed at Milliken's suggestion as witness to the other signatures.

Johnson and the deputies then loaded the boxes into the two cars they had come in and drove off to Goodland. Jamie, Dick and Milliken went into the house and sat down around the large dining room table.

"I'll be heading back myself, now," Milliken said. "I'll need to take your copy of the sheriff's inventory along in order to include it in the revised probate petition. I can have everything ready in my office for your signature by Wednesday."

"I'll be there, Mr. Milliken," Jamie said.

After Milliken had left, Jamie and Dick remained at the dining table. Jamie brought coffee and what remained of the sandwiches.

"I guess there's only one thing left I don't understand," Thatcher said. "I can't figure out how your grandfather and Dr. Black managed to periodically move a part of the treasure from the original site to the safe in the cellar without anyone seeing them and without leaving traces of their digging."

"It seems to me," Jamie said, "that the location must be significant. After all, people dig in gardens. They spade and they hoe and otherwise disturb the soil. To see someone digging out there would probably not attract attention. Their activity would have been limited to winter or early spring, though, before the garden was planted."

Thatcher nodded agreement. "That still doesn't explain how they got the job done without being seen. It really doesn't matter, I guess. Just somethng I wish I understood."

Annie came in from the kitchen carrying a fresh pot of coffee. "I thought maybe you would want a second cup," she said. "And Miss Jamie, could I talk to you and Mr. Thatcher a minute?"

"Surely, Annie," Jamie said. "Sit down and join us."

"Thanks. I ain't one to eavesdrop. Never have been. But I couldn't help hearing what you and Mr. Thatcher were saying a few minutes ago. I thought I better tell you what I know.

"Two years ago along about the end of March, Mr. Ballantine and Miss Ruth spent a weekend in town. There was some sort of social event and Miss Ruth got an invite to it. She stayed Saturday night at a friend's house and Mr. Ballantine got a room at the hotel. I went along and stayed at my sister Jenny's house. Dr. Black came out here to look after things as usual. When we got back on Sunday afternoon, I seen right away that somebody had been spading in the garden. I said something and Dr. Black said he had done the spading. Gave him something useful to do, he said, and anyway he needed the exercise. I didn't think nothing more about it. After all, it was time to get the garden ready for planting and any spading he did, I wouldn't have to do."

"Were there any other times when something like that happened, Annie?" Thatcher asked.

"I'm not real sure, Mr. Thatcher, but a year earlier, nineteen-ought-nine it would have been, Mr. Ballantine and Miss Ruth went to Fort Worth for several days. I don't remember why. Mr. Ballantine insisted I go in to Goodland while they was gone. We didn't have an automobile then and it took a long day by horse and buggy.

"Dr. Black he came out here like always. It took him all day, too. Was about the same time of the year just before time to plant the garden. I don't remember that he did any digging but he could have.

"They was other funny things happened, too, before that. I never paid any mind to them then but now I can see that each time it must have been planned so Dr. Black could be alone out here. So he could do his digging and cover his tracks. It was always just before spring planting time or in the fall after frost had finished the garden."

"I wonder," Jamie said, "how they managed it when the ranch was operating, before grandmother's death. There would have been a foreman and several ranch hands around all the time."

"Probably," Dick suggested, "during the cattle drive. There would have been one each year, most likely. To take cattle ready for market to the railroad pens at Goodland, all the ranch hands would have been needed and they would have been gone at least four days, more likely five or six. Only your grandparents and Dr. Black would have been around. Annie and Ruth weren't working at Bien Escondido yet."

"It all seems simple and logical, looking back at it," Jamie said. "Everything has an explanation. They couldn't dispose of all of it at once. It would have attracted too much attention. And they couldn't open the treasure hole frequently. They had to do it only once every year or two and then only when circumstances were just right. I'm glad you spoke up, Annie. You did the right thing. You're a true friend."

"Thanks, Miss Jamie. I'm right proud to be your friend. You're like Mr. Ballantine. He always treated me as one of the family and not just hired help. And now, if you don't mind, I think I'll go and lie down for a while. I can't remember when I've been so tired. Too much excitement, I guess."

As Annie left the room, Jamie turned to Thatcher. "Walk with me, Dick. To the lake."

Both deep in thought, they moved slowly down the path. As they approached the lake, Jamie spoke.

"I guess you know we're going to have to make some decisions. I came out here from Missouri to spend a quiet summer with grandfather Ballantine. He's gone, now. I stayed on because I got caught up in the puzzle of Bien Escondido. Now that's solved, too. And there is nothing to keep me in this lonely house. When I first saw this place I felt a strong premonition of disaster and reinforced it with a horrible nightmare. I want to get away, Dick, I really do."

"I understand, Jamie. There's no reason for me to remain, either. Certainly not if you're leaving. What I came to find — Maximilian's treasure lying down a line from three pointer rocks — is gone, too. But, Jamie," he said, suddenly taking both her hands, "I'm richer for having found you than if I had all the buried treasures in the world."

She put both arms around him quickly and pulled herself fiercely against him. She heard his voice, tenderly, softly, almost lost in the tossing waves of her hair. "I haven't said it before, Jamie," he was whispering, "I guess maybe I wanted to be sure. Today I'm sure, as certain as I could possibly be. I love you deeply and I want you more than anything I can imagine."

It was true, she thought, as their lips met in tender warmth. He had never expressed his love in words but his eyes had sent a message many times. He pulled away from her now, placing both hands on her shoulders, waiting a long moment before speaking.

"Do you think you could be happy with life in a small college town in east Texas?"

"That sounds like a proposal of marriage," Jamie said, her eyes twinkling. "And before you have a chance to claim that you were only testing the temperature of the water with your toe, I'm going to say yes.

Yes! Yes! I love you too, Dick, with all my heart! I'd marry you this afternoon if we had a preacher handy."

"That we don't have, I'm afraid. Something else, too. No ring. I can't give you a ring to seal our engagement."

"Will this do?" Jamie said, reaching into her jacket pocket and producing a massive, plain gold band. "I swiped it from poor Carlota's jewel chest when Johnson wasn't looking. I had a special reason," she said, eyes dancing. "Do you know what year this is? Nineteen-twelve. Divisible by four. A leap year. If you hadn't asked me, I'd have asked you this very afternoon. For two reasons: First because I do truly love you and second because we swore on a kiss to be partners.

"It just wouldn't be right for me to cheat my partner out of his half of the treasure, especially since I wouldn't even have known of it without his help. This way our marriage will make an honest woman of me and everything in the sheriff's sealed boxes will be half yours."

"You never cease to astonish me," Dick said as he tenderly slid the ring onto Jamie's finger. "And look, it fits perfectly. A good sign, wouldn't you say?"

Holding hands they returned to the house. They would ask Annie to join them, tell her the news, and then celebrate the engagement by opening a bottle of John Bowie Ballantine's favorite brandy.

"And you are to move out of that wretched, lonely bunkhouse this very evening," Jamie said. "Bring your things over to the main house. You can have grandfather's room. It's not where I really want you, understand, but at the moment it's the best we can do."

By late evening, the plans were set. They would drive in to Goodland tomorrow, contact the Reverend Jackson after church services and ask him to marry them that afternoon.

CHAPTER 29

Bien Escondido, Tuesday, June 22, 1912.

As I sit at the desk by the east window of this room looking out across the lake and up to distant Castle Gap, I realize with a twinge of sadness that these are the last lines I will write in my diary from here. When I leave tomorrow morning, I will close the chapter known as Bien Escondido.

I have been married to Dick Thatcher for just an hour and twenty minutes more than two days now and I do not believe my feet have yet touched the ground. Surely such great happiness, such perfect contentment, cannot last forever, but if only a quarter of it remains a year from now, I shall consider myself the most fortunate of women.

We were married last Sunday afternoon in Goodland by the Reverend Jackson. Annie and Mrs. Jackson were witnesses. Tomorrow we take the train for Fort Worth, then on to Dick's college town. House hunting is our first priority since all he has now is a bachelor apartment.

Before taking the train, we will stop at Mr. Milliken's office so I can sign the new probate petition. He says that other things I might need to sign can be handled by mail.

We have spent hours sorting grandfather's personal things and have put everything we want to keep in one room. Mr. Milliken will send men later this week to crate these things to ship to us as soon as we get settled. Everything else in the house and buildings will be sold as soon as the estate will permit. The Oldsmobile, too.

As soon as the estate is ready for closing, we are to come back out to Goodland and at that time take formal possession of the Maximilian treasure. Some of the jewelry I want to keep, but I imagine we will consign the rest of it to a qualified dealer, perhaps in New Orleans, who can sell it for us on a commission basis.

Annie has had two job offers and will have no problems. I shall remember her with fondness.

Bien Escondido! I have not yet made up my mind. I probably should sell it as soon as I have title, but do not know if I can bring myself to do so with both grandfather and grandmother buried here. It is as he said; they are part of the land. It is a decision I shall have to make later.

The sun is setting now. The lake is in early twilight, the shadows climbing Castle Mountain. But Castle Gap itself still glows and calls softly to me down the old stage road. When I first came here, only five short weeks ago, its voice was sinister, and I felt it as a threat. But I know now that it was not a threat but a challenge. The challenge of Castle Gap. I accepted that challenge. And I have won.